Town of Angels

Town of Angels

Jody Sharpe

Published by Jody Sharpe

Publisher: Jody Sharpe

Cover Design: Jody Sharpe

Back Cover Design: Jody Sharpe

Originally published in the USA by Jody Sharpe

For Elizabeth and Michael
In Memory of Norma Rivlin

If you knew who walked with you at all times on this path
that you've chosen, you could never experience
fear or doubt again.

Wayne D. Dyer (1940-2015)

Chapter 1
Angels and Butterflies

I was sent to work as a football coach for the San Francisco Shakers. I claimed to come from Botswana, Africa and everyone thinks it's true because of my accent. It is true in a way as I started my angel life helping in Botswana one hundred or so years ago. I later moved on to Kenya and coached sports teams. My fellow angel who everyone thinks is my cousin, Taylor Msumba, co-materialized to Botswana with me. No one has delved into my background or his. I materialized to San Francisco because sportsmanship was lacking in the NFL teams. I was known in my years coaching for my giant size. My quiet demeanor and my ability to promote team sportsmanship became recognized. During my career Taylor Msumba and I encouraged many to help us form a sports program for underprivileged children. Sometimes people need us so much we have to swoop in, fly down and make a difference. There seems to be so much work to do on the planet today.

Taylor and I were drawn to live in Mystic Bay, California. Yes, it's a seaside picturesque town where psychics and ordinary folk live harmoniously but there was another reason. The town's people seemingly to us angels are kind beyond the norm. To angels, kindness to others is the most beautiful expression of love. Mystic Bay is our true Earth home. Taylor lives with his wife and children. I am raising my recently adopted seven-year-old son, Val. I love my role as an angel living a human life. There are a seven of us in Mystic Bay, yet no one knows this secret. When I met the young orphan, Val, I found his troubled past unthinkable. It was a reason to stay. He needed me and now my life as his father will take me living long into the human life. I will go back to heaven aging like all angels living as humans do. I'll go back to my angel calling helping others in need around the world. Will I be an old looking angel then? I don't know for that is another secret of life and heaven.

This Mystic Bay town of seven angels is special also because last summer other heavenly angels appeared to three children with disabilities here. This event caused a worldwide phenomenon spreading love and joy, so needed on the planet. July North, one of the town's resident angels and a famous talk show host, introduced the world to the miraculous story.

Justine Greer is another reason I stay. Her twins, Mike and Liz have been her light and reason to move forward since last summer. For as the sea winds blew gently through the open screen door of *The Painted Butterfly*, Justine's store, their late father, her husband, called her. The amazing part of it was Ned had been gone to the Heaven Realm for weeks but there his voicemail was in a whispering sound as if catching his breath. Ned whispered, "Hi, have a good day, love you..." Justine told me she felt like an electric current pierced through her clairsensitive body. She explained how she sat and cried for hours listening to the message over and over again until she had to stop. Their last conversation lay like flowers on her broken heart, for the day he passed away they had spoken of their love for each other. She thought it was their final goodbye but when she heard his voice she knew Ned's spirit wanted to comfort her and their children by letting them know he was safe in the Heaven Realm.

I know her story very well for I've been a part of her life from the beginning. Justine knows me as her dearest friend, Ken Leighton, her across the street neighbor of ten years now. But in reality I have another role. I have been her guardian angel all her life. I've watched Justine, a psychic girl from Mystic Bay grow into the kind and good woman she is and the gifted artist who paints butterflies. With angels wind, I've swirled butterflies her way on the sweetest days of her life. I hold out my hand and angel wind forms swirling so butterflies instantly appear fluttering. It makes my angel heart sing to the heavens with joy watching the delight on her face.

I materialized on Earth as a human to help those in need. I actually thought I'd go back to Heaven's Realm after my first fly down years ago as we angels call it, but I had to stay. Justine and her children have had such sad expressions this lonely year without Ned. His unexpected call from heaven brightened their world, yes, but their grief is still so painful especially as they were all so close to Ned. Their extended family and friends like me have tried to fill their life with as many good times as possible this long year.

We seven angels residing in this little town by the sea are drawn to help our wonderful folks. Some of the people in town here have psychic abilities and some don't. We angels live amongst them, materializing in physical form. Three of the angels here are married to humans and one is widowed. But my story is about our work and lives here as angels living a human life. Sometimes people need us so much we have to swoop in, fly down and make a difference. I am here for the long haul now as Val's father. His troubled past was unthinkable. He needed me and now my life as his father will take me living long into the human life.

Val and I walk into *The Painted Butterfly*, my morning ritual for coffee, which I love, and exchange morning greetings with Justine. With a "good morning" she hugs my new son. Her long chestnut hair is swept up in a ponytail, her big blue eyes sparkle a little more than I've seen in a year and her smile is infectious. The hurt is disappearing from her face little by little. Her small rescue poodle mix, Walnut, runs to us like a dust mop on tiny legs. Val bends down to embrace him. "Well, a happy greeting for us, Justine. Good morning my favorite girl and Happy Birthday to you as well! May it be a great day and year for you!"

"Happy Birthday," Val adds his big brown eyes shining a little more than usual I notice.

"Thank you both! Yes, it's a going to be a fun day, Ken. I'm so glad you and Val are coming tonight for the party at Mom and Dads'. The twins and their friends will be there and we invited Angie and Ricky as well."

"Terrific!" My new store managers, Angie and Ricky are young just marrieds who moved to town recently. "After I retired, I bought the building next door to Justine and her parents, and opened an angel gift shop called, Heaven Can't Wait. On the top floor of her building Bob, Justine's Dad, has a tax and accounting firm that he's selling.

Justine's younger brother, Bobby, also has opened his own law practice there. While at a big law firm in San Francisco, he had a brief and troubled end to a romance with his boss's daughter. Bobby needed to get away to start anew back in his hometown of Mystic Bay.

"Bring Barty to play with Walnut too. The more dogs the merrier, " Justine laughs and it's good to hear her laugh again.

" I will if our Barty isn't taking one of his many naps."

" Val, wait to you see the cake Laurjean is making!"

"Wow, yeah," Val says still playing with Walnut. I look at Justine and a mist-filled moment of remembering a long ago day fills the room yet only my angel eyes can see it. Angels can see memories. Val and Justine are playing with Walnut but I can see the vividness of yesterday. *Justine had just turned six and I thought it time to send the first yellow butterfly to land on her shoulder. She was sitting on the porch of her childhood home. Her parents still live in the same house down the street from her. She was drawing pretty flowers on a notebook pad as I sent on angel wind a small butterfly. I knew instantly it would impact her life. I was near but above her and sent a butterfly from the garden. I whispered to it to land on dear little Justine's shoulder. She didn't move a muscle. Her eyes glanced at it without moving her head. The butterfly flew away but her artistic talent focused on drawing butterflies and she began to draw and paint them.* The mist clears. I think of how Pam Ellen, her mother, began painting and drawing butterflies too and soon their house was filled with butterflies.

The day Justine met Ned was another day I sent her butterflies. Another mist filled moment fills the room but Justine and Val are still engaged with Walnut and don't notice. *Justine is sitting on the grass waiting for class at UCLA. She is daydreaming about the future drawing her butterflies on her notepad. A young man comes up to her, pens and notebook in hand. It is Ned. "Excuse me miss, you have a butterfly on your shoulder!" Justine gazes up at the cute guy, looks down at the butterfly and says, "Oh, wow, I didn't notice but yes, they come to me and rest only on the sweetest of days!" She shyly turns away knowing he will ask the next question. "Would you like to have coffee after class with me?"* The mist lifts and once again I am back in the present moment.

Twenty years later, Justine and Ned had made a beautiful life together in the town she grew up in. She and Ned would open the store in the building her dad and mom owned. She and her mom would paint everything butterfly. Bob and Ned made all the furniture to paint. With butterfly vases, candleholders and plates, they soon had their dream life.

Then Justine gave birth to their wonderful twins. Life seemed nearly perfect in Mystic Bay where psychics and ordinary folk live, where angels found their way to reside. But when Ned became ill her world changed to caregiving for him. She's learning one of life's most valuable lessons that the now is all there is.

She looks at me now while she makes more coffee. "Ken, I want to thank you for introducing your CPA, Mac Jones to Dad and Bobby. Mac is signing the papers to take over Dad's business today. Dad's ecstatic to retire. Bobby helped Mac adopt his granddaughter. We're going to celebrate a lot of things tonight including the twins leaving for college. I'd like Mac and his granddaughter to come over to the party if they'd like. Lots of good things today, I guess. What would we have ever done if you hadn't moved to town and bought *Heaven Can't Wait?*" Your friendship means everything to me." I smile telling her I feel the same way.

Mac Jones is my accountant. I met him in my football coaching days and he does taxes now for my store. I introduced him to Bobby who helped him adopt his granddaughter in a long battle for custody. Val's adoption was easier as no one contested it. He was a lonely child in a group home and wasn't being placed. I felt compelled to adopt him.

"Wait til you meet Mac and his little granddaughter, Billie Jo. He's a great guy. Billie Jo and Val are the same age and since Mac rented the other half of my duplex, Val will have a friend to play with and walk to the bus stop." Val nods smiling. Happiness seems contagious this morning.

Mike and Liz walk in. "Happy Birthday Mom, hi Ken and Val," they almost say in unison." Justine's twins give her big hugs. Liz hands their mom a bouquet from them.

"Thanks guys, these are so beautiful!"

Mike states," Hey. Grandma wants us to pick up Laurjean's cake, ice and get more lettuce for the salads. Anything we can help you with Mom? It's your day all day!"

"I'm doing all the flowers for the party, daisies like these I think," Liz explains bending down to see Val and Walnut playing. She's the spitting image of her mom, tall and statuesque with those sparkling blue eyes. Mike looks like a younger version of Ned, tall, dark and handsome. His eyes twinkle as he looks at his mom. Liz and he both inherited the psychic gene from their mother and grandmother.

Liz, will pursue the healing arts in college as she already has proven to have a gift with Reiki. She will be a notable healer in the future, her mom and grandmother predict. Mike sees the spirits of dogs and cats near their people. Yet his abilities go far beyond that.

I look around the imaginative butterfly store as the conversation continues about our celebratory dinner and my heart sings again. Yes, life is good. Val is getting more secure living with me and I'm hoping he'll feel comfortable enough to call me 'Dad' someday, as his restless nights lessen. My heart aches for him yet I see improvements with the help of a wonderful child psychologist that Mac Jones referred me to.

"Someone will be walking to the front door in a moment, Justine informs us, her very psychic ability alert is typical. She knows when people are walking towards her door, some days she knows who they are. We all turn to see the tall kind man, Mac Jones and his granddaughter walking up to the screen door of the store. I explain, "It's Mac Jones, Justine." She meets him at the door. "Hi Mac, I'm Bob's daughter, Justine Greer."

"Hello, Mac Jones, I've heard a lot about you from your dad, Justine. This is my granddaughter, Billie Jo." The little girl turns her head into her grandfather's waist. "Your dad said to meet him here." Mac is such a wonderful man and Billie Jo is blessed to finally live with him. Val has met her a few times and likes her. Her mother has mental health issues but had a hard time letting go of her daughter. It finally ended a few months ago when her mother signed the papers. Billie Jo's grandmother, Mac's late wife, Vicky, would be so happy he told me for it was her dream to adopt this child.

Mac and Billie Jo's introductions are made. Bob quickly comes down the stairs from the upper office of Mystic Bay CPA to greet him. "Welcome, Mac and of course you too little Billie Jo." He pats her on the head saying, " So very happy to see you here. Have you met everyone?"

"Yes, we have." Bobby comes down the stairs of the upper floor offices too. He looks a lot like his father, broad shouldered, muscular sort of like me only I'm the biggest man in town.

" Hey, Mac and Billie Jo. I am thrilled you're here!"

Bob remarks, "We can sign the papers upstairs. I know you're moving in today and have movers coming so it won't take long. Our transition will be smooth and I will stay as long as you need me to get you off to a good start. We'll help you move in too."

Mac smiles, "You are too kind and I thank you for that." Liz offers to take Val and Billie Jo to the "kids corner," the little area in the store where there are lots of toys and soft cloth butterflies to play with. Justine has set up a terrific play area for the kids. Billie Jo looks at Mac with pleading eyes. "Can I, Grandpa?"

"Of course you can go, Sweetie," he tells her in a gentle voice. Liz takes the kids by the hands and off they go to the area set up for kids to enjoy while the parents shop. Billie Jo is a small fragile fair-haired girl whose face has a worried look yet I see beginnings of a spark of hope's light in her eyes.

I know Mac. He is an exceptional man thrown into the sadness of losing his wife and fighting for custody of his stepdaughter's child at the same time. When the children are in the other area Bob and Mac say their goodbyes, but as they turn to walk up the stairs Mike stops them. "Excuse me, Mac." He turns to make sure the children are engaged with Liz and the toys. In a low voice he continues, " I have a feeling Grand Dad has told you of our psychic town and maybe that my mom and Grandma are psychics or sensitives as some say?"

"Well yes, Mike. Your grandfather did tell me all about the town and the psychics and the angels sightings."

Mike looks at Justine for approval and she nods her head. Then Mike continues in a soft voice. " Well, I see the spirits of pets, animal companions, who have passed. Often, I see them around their loved ones. Sometimes they stay and comfort their owners for a while. Your little granddaughter has a white fluffy puppy near her. She sees her in her dreams."

Mac is speechless. His hand moves to the banister to steady himself.

I place my hand on his arm to calm him. Mac says in a quiet voice, "Oh. Yes, there is a story behind that, a sad one. One to share another time." Billie Jo runs up to her grandpa from the kid's corner. "Look Grandpa what Liz gave me? It's a yellow butterfly, can I keep it?"

Mac bends down to see, "Of course, Sweetie! How nice, and your favorite color too! Thank you, Liz!" He smiles a winning smile. Everyone engages in watching Billie Jo but I watch Justine. There are tears in her eyes. She pictures long ago events of other people's lives she's told me. These events are sometimes sad ones that explain an action or words.

Bob smiles, "Mac you and Billie Jo are going to like it here. Mystic Bay is a good town, good people and no shortage of love and butterflies or angels in this town. And we have the Pacific Ocean too. What else could you need?" Billie Jo tugs at her grandfathers pant leg. In a sad voice, "Can I have a dog like Walnut? I miss Coco, my dog." Mac hugs her. "As soon as we're settled in, I promise." Billie Jo's face brightens.

We say goodbye, as I will take Billie Jo home with Val and me so Mac can have his meeting with Bob. Then the movers will be here. It's a busy day in Mystic Bay, with new beginnings for everyone. Justine stops us, "Wait. Mac would you and Billie Jo like to have dinner at my parents' home tonight? They live right down the street from you and Ken can bring you. We're having a party and I'm sure it would be fun for Billie Jo to be with Val and Walnut too! You can meet some of our friends."

Bob interjects, "Why didn't I think of that. Yes, Mac please join us?"

"Well sure, we'd love that wouldn't we Billie Jo?"

I sure love watching over my flock. There's light starting to shine again in Justine's eyes today. Even the twin's eyes are shining again. Opening the screen door to leave I decide today on Justine's forty-seventh birthday I'll send some butterflies as she leaves the shop. Maybe it will help her start painting again. Butterflies are truly God's tiniest joys on earth.

~~~~~~~~~~

At the party, it was wonderful to see Justine laugh and have fun. When she opened her cards she read each one out loud. Most were funny ones but when she opened the twins' butterfly card her eyes misted up as she read the heartwarming and loving sentiments:

Dear Mom,

I know this year has been hard but I want you to know how proud I am of you. You still have your wings, and you'll fly again soon. Happy Birthday! Love, Mike

Happy Birthday Mom,

I love this Proverb…

Just when the caterpillar thought the world had ended, it became a butterfly…

Love, Liz

It's past his bedtime on the star-filled summer night as Val and I walk home hand in hand next to Mac and Billie Jo. The party was grand, the lasagna consumed and to top it off Laurjean's cake has filled me up so much, I better watch my waistline! We say goodnight as Mac and Billie walk into their side of the duplex, their furniture inside and beds made thanks to all our efforts of help. They must be exhausted. Barty, my old dog, appears to greet us. Still enthusiastic, he almost bowls Val over. He and Val have the new bond of boy and dog. We climb the stairs and get in PJ's,
~~~~~~~~~~

brush our teeth together and have story time. Val's reading abilities are getting better and we each read a few pages of his book. We say our prayers as Barty snores lying at the side of the bed. "I love you to the moon and back," I say softly looking at my dear child. We love to gaze at the moon each night thanking God for the day. "Me too," my precious son replies. I stay until he falls asleep, as has been our routine since he came to stay. Barty knows instinctively he's to stay with Val each night now for it comforts the boy. Our angel spirits know a broken spirit can be renewed through love. Love can repair any emotion. When his eyes tell me he's sleeping, I tiptoe into my own room and pick up the book on parenting that the psychologist recommended. No, angels don't know everything and we learn so much from our humans. We guide yet, learn.

I read by the light of the moon as I always do for angels can read in near dark. Yawning now with the sleep of an angel human, I place my head down loving the softness of the pillow. Yes, my life is good here. Being a father has been exhausting and exhilarating at the same time. Helping others is our path, my path. As the lights turn off in the houses in my little seaside town and the streetlights brighten, I thank Him. "Give me wisdom, help me take the best road for Val." I won't go back to the heaven realm until I'm aged and gray, the way of many angels around the world having a human experience. Will I tell Val the truth about me someday? Heaven I know will deem it so.

Justine, Mac and their children will sleep peacefully tonight as will Bob, Pam Ellen and Bobby. A new day has started for them all. Yes, I'll fly tomorrow night with my angel friends and we will once again soar over the many rooftops of the kindest of towns, Mystic Bay, where angels live as humans and no one knows the secret.

Chapter 2
Seven Angels

We fly every Saturday night. The first to land in town was Angel Gabe O'Ryan who owns Dear Dogs Etc. with his daughter, Hannah. He lost his dear wife many years ago but has raised Hannah, a half angel, well and now she is married to our second angel, Doc Josh Ryder, our veterinarian. They are blessed with little twins now. They both have angel gifts with animals and their mission is to save as many as they can and because of them our town has embraced rescuing.

The third angel is Taylor Msumba, who is supposedly my cousin and Botswana native like me. He works for Gabe as bookkeeper and manager.

Our newest additions, Angel July North, our resident famous talk show host and her sister, January, are such lovely angels. July came to town a few years ago for a TV show and fell in love with the town. Her sister followed.

Last but not least our big Native American angel, Donnie Whitefeather, Laurjean's husband. They own The Next Door Café. His story of helping his tribe overcome alcoholism epitomizes what an angel dusting of love can do. As a boy he came to the tribe and miracles took place. These angels are my friends, my confidents. Yes, we all are unlikely looking angels but that's the beauty of it. Only the spouses and some of our children know the secret. And that's the way it needs to be.

However, a few years back our secret almost became national news. In a moment of emotional weakness, Hannah, told her ex-

13

boyfriend and creative writing professor, Sam Blakley, the truth about her father, Gabe. They broke up. In retaliation though not believing it was true, he penned a novel hinting there was a real female angel living as a human in California. With her likeness on the book cover and hints she was a real angel the story went viral. The media swarmed into town. Yet Hannah kept the secret safe with July North's help. July exposed the author as a cad looking to make money from his novel. His life made a slight change when he apologized to Hannah on July's TV show.

Angels living on earth have lots of work to do but tonight when we fly we will see cascading stars and picture perfect milky moonlight. For flying fills us with the love of Earth and the beautiful people we care for. Looking up to silvery clouds and misty star-filled skies brings a peace all its own. Closer to heaven, I always think while flying.

Our Saturday has been a good day. Val and Billie Jo played at my house as Mac worked with Bob in the office. Pam Ellen and Bob invited us all over for leftovers from the party and we had a more quiet evening with their family. Mac and Billie Jo were invited too. The children are each in their own separate homes as slumber comes but my night is just beginning. When the two angels enter the room, Barty opens one eye then closes it; his long tail wags slowly and even.

Without words only thoughts, January sits beside Val's bed smiling at the beautiful child's face in slumber. She will babysit Val as a few of us fly tonight. January's angel sister, July, is at home with Heather, her adopted child. We take turns babysitting each other's children. Yes, some angels living as humans in Mystic Bay are following the call of many folks in town by adopting children.

Instantly, Gabe and I are on the roof. Angel Gabe is a jolly angel who thirty years ago flew to save a lovely young woman, Kate, from an oncoming car. They instantly fell in love. He was the first angel here to ask heaven for a chance to be human.

We sit for a moment admiring the night sky in anticipation. "Now that I have Val to care for, you'll help me tell him about me one day when the timing is right?"

"Of course Ken. I told Hannah when she was too young, though. Everything went along fine until she told the secret I was an angel to her boyfriend, Sam Blakley and he subsequently wrote the novel *My California Angel*. Thank goodness, everything has calmed down. Chris knows his father, our dear Donnie, is an angel, and he himself is half angel but he waited til Chris was in high school to tell him. According to Donnie, Chris has never told anyone. Chris flew with Donnie as a child too but Donnie would sprinkle him with angel dust when they got home and the next day Chris always thought he'd dreamed of flying. Remember, Madam Norma's great granddaughter; Maggie and her husband Noah Greenstreet saw us fly together during the eclipse last year because they are both amazing psychics? But what happened next is well and good."

"Oh yes, but tell me again, I so love the story?"

"You remember, on they're honeymoon, Angel Josh, my dear son in law, followed my suggestion. He flew to their honeymoon spot off Long Island. Josh sprinkled a wind of angel dust lightly as they slept. They woke up almost forgetting it really happened and wondering if seeing us flying that night was all a dream. Even now when I see them in town they talk to me as if nothing happened and that's a good thing." Gabe laughs, "No, Ken, there is always angel dust to sprinkle if things go awry. Now they are sure they dreamed the same dream."

"The secret that we are angels is safe for now, Gabe, but I will wait til Val is older. It must be wondrous to take your children with you flying overlooking the town we love." Gabe raises his hands to heaven with a resounding, "Amen! Let's fly now so I can get back home for my beauty rest!" We two angels laugh spreading sparkling wings made of stardust, feathers and sunshine.

We fly up into the early September night sky. We will fly away from the quaint houses and off to Mystic Bay Harbor. The mist from the Pacific is like heavy velvet now but that doesn't bother us. This is peace, the flying at night when no one can see us or hear us talking. Val won't awaken, as his slumber is deep. Above the milky moon moves higher, the mist becoming thicker.

We swoop down seeing our dear friend in town, Jamie Bond, below walking his dog. We call him the 'comeback kid' for all the strides he's made improving his life. Jamie doesn't see us of course but his small shepherd mix Bondo does. All God's special creatures can see angels just fine. The dog stops and stares. Jamie stops, looks up, doesn't see anything but the beauty of the misty night and encourages Bondo to keep walking. Jamie opens the door to climb the stairs to his apartment above *Mystic Bay Wine and Cheese*.

Jamie is a young success story. He soon will open his own bike store. Psychics, Madam Norma and her daughter, Miss Marilyn changed his life by improving his self esteem and teaching him the skills necessary to dutifully help raise his daughter.

Tim, Miss Marilyn's husband, gave him a job at *Mystic Bay Wine and Cheese* and now with their financial help he's opening his dream, his store in town called *Bondo's Bikes*. Through the psychic and healing art of persuasion, Madam Norma worked her beautiful magic. Jamie Bond is a changed man and responsible for his daughter, Emma Rose, who has intellectual disabilities. He also helps support now the mother of his child, Elena, who's a college student. Emma Rose is the child who was mute but spoke for the first time when she saw an angel last year. Her first word was 'angel'. It was one of those miracles of life, the dear heaven sent miracles.

"Glory Hallelujah," I shout as we fly near Laurjean and Donnie's house. Angel Donnie Whitefeather is on the roof and flies meeting us with bright golden wings, the shiniest wings of any angels living as a human in Mystic Bay. We nod a greeting and keep on soaring toward the sea over the harbor. A few boat lights shimmer on the water but no one sees us. Swooshing down to the waves, we three angels delight in the sea spray misting our faces. Our soft wings repel the water as all feathered creatures do. Our wings disappear when we come down again to live our human existence. We meet up with angels, Doc Josh and Taylor. We never say much just nodding and smiling at each other. The feelings bring speechless wonder to our angelness. We glide feeling wind yet neither heat nor cold. If it rains, we only feel a mist envelope us.

The twinkling lights of town start calling us back to our homes. This is our weekly ritual, if weather permits and someone can babysit the kids. Gabe waves goodbye to Donnie as he lands on his roof with bird like precision. The golden wings fall to his side then disappear. Laurjean is on the roof to greet her husband. Approaching my roof we see Bondo, the dog, looking out the lighted window of Jamie's second story apartment. His paws on the windowsill, he gazes at us in wonder as if we are giant birds. Gabe waves and the dog notices. Jamie looks out the window to find out what Bondo is looking at. He can't see us of course so he shuts the window and I chuckle to myself. Lighting on the roof, our iridescent wings disappear. January joins us for late conversation.

January says in a soft voice, "Val is sound asleep and Barty is watching, I know he won't awaken."

"Thank you, dear. You can fly next time. I'll ask Justine to babysit Heather and Val. July and I already have it planned so we can all fly together. Val is comfortable with Justine and it's time he tried a sleep over. He loves little Heather. By the way, Madam Norma told Gabe and me a problem is coming to town. We are planning to meet soon."

Gabe points out, "Oh it's unfortunate but the town will rise to the occasion as always. Another of life's lessons."

The lovely angel January, says her goodnight, lifts her milky moon white wings into the night flying to her home near the *Sea Watch Hotel* to her sister July and July's little Heather. Her graceful glide is breathtaking. As he does at the end of our flying Gabe asks, "Tell me something good, Ken." Gabe's eyes twinkle merrily mirroring the lights of town at night.

"My life here on earth being Val's father is a blessing. I embraced my work with my fellow football players and can still guide my flock. Yet, giving Val all the fatherly love he's always deserved, well".... Choked up I have to stop. "How did you manage it, Gabe? How do you go on without your lovely wife Kate, all these long years?"

Gabe puts his hand on my shoulder. "When you fall in love in the Earth Realm, you have to think beyond to the moment of total reunion, the most glorious of days. I still see Kate's spirit so I know when it's time I'll go to her and we will soar together. But now I have to love my daughter, and my precious grandchildren, my family. There's work to be done on Earth, Ken, oh so much work to be done. With all the strife, and sadness, we angels on earth must nudge our flock towards love as much as possible. We must find a way to bring lasting peace on the most inexplicably beautiful blue planet in the Milky Way."

"Yes, all the children deserve love and protection. January will be adopting Val's cousin Spencer soon. He will be so happy when I tell him as he worries for the boy. It's been January and my plan all along to bring the boys together living as cousins in a safe trusting family environment. Billie Jo, the little girl who moved into the other duplex will do well here now with Mac, her grandfather's, guiding hands. But Gabe you know, he needed her just as much as she needed him. Funny isn't it?" Gabe smiles nodding knowing one of the secrets of life.

The angelic beauty of the streetlights glows in amber below. A jet sounds above and we turn our heads in unison to watch the jet trail move south in and out of the cloudy mist.

"All over the world some angels live briefly or longer as humans in order to watch over their people. Yes, some of us fall in love and marry and if we do we have to keep the secret safe. But for now, this is where we angels congregate, at night when no one can see us. Even if someone were taking a midnight stroll like Jamie Bond, they wouldn't be able to hear us speak."

A door opens across the street. Justine has walked outside to say goodnight to God and the sky. Walnut follows, her. Walnut looks up, seeing us on the roof. Of course he is quiet for dogs never bark at us. Justine's wrapped in her robe, arms folded. Her face looks at the misty moon. "Her life is about to change. Good things are coming her way." At that moment, we see Mac Jones walk out his front door to look at the stars and sky. With the light of the moon and streetlights they see each other and wave. They both go back into their houses shutting the doors. Gabe pats me on the shoulder, " Goodnight dear friend."

"Goodnight." He flies away with a nod and a wave to his home behind his store on Main Street. Instantly, I'm tiptoeing into Val's room finding he's sleeping soundly. His covers are up to his chin and Barty is breathing softly. One day he'll know not only I am his father, the ex football coach and owner of *Heaven Can't Wait* but surprisingly an angel living as a human in the oh so wonderful town of Mystic Bay.

Yawning in my human form, tired now for sleep, I pet Barty on the head and walk to my room again. No need to turn on the light while getting ready to have a few angel winks of human sleep. The moon softly lights the room as I get into my comfortable bed and open a book. Moonlight reading puts me to sleep. I want to read all the books on raising children I can find. I enjoy all the children's books for Val and the other kids I work with. Angels can read a book in thirty minutes usually. But my eyes can't stay open, so I put the book down on the bedside table remembering all the days when love changed the world. I drift with the memory into angelic dreamland.

Chapter 3

Madam Norma and Her Psychic Vibe

It's a beautiful Sunday in our seaside town of Mystic Bay. The sun is shining brightly; the seabirds are flying as little birds chirp their 'hello' when I open the back door to my store. Barty and I walk in. I won't open until eleven. Angie and Ricky, my managers, are off Sunday so it's my turn to work today. Barty goes to his regular dog bed by my desk and does his usual three circles before he lies down.

I make a pot of coffee for the company coming in a few minutes and look around enjoying all the plentiful angels of various sizes, shapes and colors around my store. They depict so many of the angels I have known. Down through history man has believed yet few have seen us. There are Guardian angels like me, Archangels like Michael, Gabriel, Uriel and a plethora of essential angels, healing angels, so many kinds, all so pure in thought and deed. Our love is strong and we tend the gardens of life as best we can with guidance from above. My heart aches for the flock here for trouble is brewing. Right now Justine is babysitting Val for me. Mac and Bob are hard at work going over accounts in their upstairs office. Pam Ellen will come in later so Justine can take the kids out for ice cream with Laurjean and her little boy Stevie. Taylor walks in. "Morning, my angel friend," he smiles.

"Good morning to you. How's the family? Help yourself to some coffee."

"Everything is perfect, thank you for asking. Thanks for the coffee, my man!"

"Madam Norma will be coming over in a few minutes for a conversation with us and we must make sure when she stares into our eyes we don't stare back. I'm afraid the dear old psychic is really wondering about us." Taylor's face doesn't hide the look of worry.

"Oh, now Taylor, it's been thirty years since she's known Gabe, ten years since both of our friendships started with her, you really think it's possible she figured it out?"

"I'm wondering." As if on cue the front door opens and in scoots Madam Norma in her motorized scooter with her seventy-five-year-old daughter, the lovely Miss Marilyn. Son-in -law Tim Thayer must be at his own store. "Hey guys," she says with a wave of her hand.

We go over to our favorite one hundred year old lady, the brilliant, kind and the oldest psychic in town, Madam Norma. She is the woman who changed many a life in Mystic Bay with her wisdom and psychic abilities. Charming psychicness is a favorite tool of the angels.

"Well, good morning you two." Taylor and I give each lady a kiss on the cheek.

"Good morning," Miss Marilyn says cheerily. Her psychic vibe is good but no one can compare to her mother's intuition. Madam Norma tells us, "I wanted to meet with you first before we tell Justine and Bobby this morning. Klaus Waxman, Bobby's ex-boss and Miranda's father, has rented the building next to Tim's *Mystic Bay Wine and Cheese*. He's going to open a competitor to your shop and Justine's store. He's calling it, *The Angel and Butterfly Shoppe* according to the license filed. It's going to hit Justine hard as his goal is to hurt Bobby and his family for Bobby's breaking up with Miranda. It's revenge, unfortunately. But there is something else. I don't know yet but he has another ulterior motive concerning the town. The realtor said there was no law prohibiting him from having a store name that competes with yours and

Justine's just like Tim's *Mystic Bay Wine and Cheese* and *The Package and Wine Store* on the edge of town. I'm sure you'll prevail but it will mean some chaotic times for a while for all of us. I've asked Justine and Bobby to come over to your store in a few minutes. I'll need your support for a plan I'm brewing." Madam Norma is known for her brewing plans like a cauldron of problem solving thoughts and good deeds.

"Sounds okay with us. "

"I have to think fast as Jamie's new store is on the other side between *Mystic Bay Wine and Cheese* and the new store and I'll try to keep Jamie's vigilante personality from doing anything rash. Klaus is going to promote his store with a big opening the same day as Jamie's next Saturday. He'll sell all kinds of butterflies and angels also to hurt Justine and ultimately you, Ken. I don't know the man at all, but he's not on a good plane right now. So I want you both to be here with your gentleness and guiding ways. Taylor and I look at each other for a moment. Does she know about us? My angelness says she wonders about us for sure. "I'm asking Gabe O'Ryan, Josh, July and January North to come over to *Bondo's Bikes* Grand Opening too since you all are friends and have calming effects on people. And well, let me just say Klaus is going to come into Jamie's store that very day and try to make a scene."

Taylor and I don't look at each other this time but I'm sure both his eyes look away for a moment as do mine. When I look back at the little old darling psychic she winks or does she? Wow, this is unbelievable. All these years we have never suspected anyone knew about us except her great granddaughter, Maggie and her husband, Noah, on the night of the eclipse. Did they tell her? We think not. Now if Madam Norma doesn't really know, well, is she guessing? Taylor speaks quickly, "Right Madam Norma. We will be there for sure." I look at Miss Marilyn and can tell she may be psychic but is clueless about us angels.

Justine and Bobby walk in smiling their hellos. Bobby has a

skip in his step now that he's in business for himself. No more Klaus Waxman or Miranda Waxman to worry about he thinks. My heart twinges as Madam Norma begins.

"Can we sit at this table, Ken? This will only take a moment or two."

Bobby asks, "Madam Norma, is this meeting about Jamie's store opening? We want to help if we can with flyers, food, whatever you all need."

"No, but thank you, Bobby. We are all set for next Saturday. No there is another issue to discuss." Bobby and Justine have quizzical looks on their faces. " You see, Bobby, Klaus Waxman has rented the building across the street next to Tim's and to *Bondo's Bikes*. I'm afraid both of you will be upset. He's opening *The Angels and Butterfly Shoppe*. I'm certain it's in retaliation for you breaking up with Miranda. You and I have talked about the possibility. But all will be all right in the end, I'm sure of it. He's got other ulterior motives, I'm sure, but we will beat him at the pass as the old cowboys I knew used to say ninety years ago."

Bobby looks at Justine and takes her hand. Justine starts, "This is really extreme. I'm confident in my products and sales but to move to town and sell angels and butterflies right across the street? I'm shocked I didn't see this one coming." Bobby seems more worried which is something I didn't expect. "Miranda is spoiled and aggressive like her dad. I was a fool to go out with her. She put up a good front and fooled me for a while but I'm not as surprised if I think about it. Revenge is second nature to the Waxman family. To bad the mother is not living. Although the mother seems a forbidden subject." Bobby puts his arm around Justine.

"Bobby, this town needs you as the good lawyer in town that you are and no one is going to let him do anything. Why my late husband was a hometown lawyer and good to people and you are too. He never took anything lying down. We'll get through this but I'm worried Klaus wants to hurt your name, your sister's business, and your reputation by spreading lies. What I find most peculiar is why he wants to sell angels, Ken? This is very vengeful and I so wish I could stand up straight to him. But I have to do it from my scooter now. He's Grand Opening his store next Saturday same day as Jamie's. People are stocking the store now getting ready. We have to be prepared for whatever he has up his sleeve." Madam Norma looks pale suddenly and it makes me worry for her for a moment. Then the color comes back in her face. Maybe she doesn't know we are angels. Maybe I'm experiencing a little human anxiety for nothing. This is not like me. Usually, I am able to handle every situation. I send angel winds of love, comfort and strength to all in the room.

Miss Marilyn joins the conversation, "The angels will protect us, they always do, Mother. We just wanted to warn you and we want Ken, Taylor and others to be at Jamie's opening for moral support in case the horrid man pulls something. We know he's going to barge in and say something."

The Angel clock strikes eleven and Madam Norma and Miss Marilyn say their goodbyes and leave. Bobby, Justine, Taylor and I stare at each other. I break the silence. "Look, it's going to be a challenge but I…"

Bobby breaks in, "It's a worry what Miranda and Klaus will do. Why are they taking such enormous steps to rent a building across from ours, have a shop that sells angels and butterflies? It's pretty severe." Bobby's hand runs through his hair. "I actually knew I'd made a mistake about the third date and I kept it going to please her dad. I didn't know how to get out of it. Finally, after two months of dating I told her I was moving back here to be a small town lawyer. I didn't want the pressure, I didn't care about the money or position as I love the down home life here. She was outraged, starting yelling saying "wasn't she beautiful enough for me…money is so important and Daddy will be mad"…. etc. I told her I was sorry, it had nothing to do with her or her looks. I walked into her dad's office an hour later. I didn't ask for back pay, just asked for the clients I brought into the firm, just the individuals I'd known before. He knew I had him there. He screamed and yelled at me that I had broken Miranda's heart. He told me to pack up and get out, not to wait for the two-week notice. He made a scene in the office. The staff and the attorneys were horrified. They told me they'd all leave if they could, but they were making good money and had families to raise. I didn't blame anybody for not sticking up for me at all. I left relieved.

Miranda wasn't for me. Justine always thought Klaus would try to get even and now Madam Norma has verified it."

Justine is upset. "Yes, but not like this. This is crazy-nuts. I can't stay, have to get back to the store and take the kids for ice cream. Bobby please join us. It'll be good to take your mind off it." She hugs me and says goodbye to Taylor. Bobby shakes our hands and leaves with her. When they've shut the door Taylor remarks sadly, "This is just too bad. These people don't deserve being harassed like this but we'll help them. Hey, do think Madam Norma is on to us? It sure seems so."

"I don't know, Taylor. I have a feeling she wonders and yet isn't sure. To play it safe we'll have to form a club, group and name it for the seven of us. She must hear we get together on Saturday nights and switch off babysitting. We need a name that sounds innocuous like Mystic Bay something, I don't know what!"

Taylor says in our Botswana accent. "We will induct January and July into our Bay Area Sports Program. July already contributes so much to us and wants to do more. They can help establish a girl's program. I'm sure they'll make time. It'll be our cover yet helps the kids too. July even expressed an interest a few weeks ago."

"Ok, sounds good." After Taylor leaves and a customer has come in to admire the angels, it's just Barty and me so I walk over to the lighted all white Christmas tree that has nothing but angel ornaments on it all year long. I love Christmas trees. I single out my favorite one. It's a little boy angel with a baseball cap and uniform. *Dads Angel* it says on the little boy's red shirt. I want to give it to Val next Christmas. My angel heart knows that the Delany and Greer families will be victorious over Klaus Waxman, I just don't know how. It's just another life challenge but something Madam Norma said strikes me, something about being more than about opening the competition store. "What can it be?"

Chapter 4

The Two Grand Openings

Today is Friday and it's been a big week in Mystic Bay. Val and Billie Jo started second grade Tuesday. Mac and I walked the kids to the bus stop and my angel sense tells me this will be a wonderful year for them. The kids get along famously and will sleepover tomorrow night at Justine's. She has accepted my request to babysit so my angel friends and I can go flying. But of course she thinks we're all going out to San Francisco to meet to discuss our Bay Area Sports Program. She'll babysit Heather North too so July and January can fly with us. All seven of us will get to fly together for the first time in months.

The Grand Opening is tomorrow also for *Bondo's Bikes* and Klaus Waxman's *The Angel and Butterfly Shoppe*. We have all had such a busy week that the thought of mean spiritedness coming to town has been put on the back burner of our thinking. Perhaps Justine's babysitting will take her mind off Klaus Waxman. Today Justine, Bobby and I are having an early breakfast at *The Next Door Café*. Laurjean has her coffeepot in hand as we decide to order pancakes. Donnie's Sunshine Pancakes are almost famous in town. Laurjean quips, as she pours, "That guy Klaus better not show his face here in our restaurant tomorrow as I might have to pour coffee in his lap." She's dyed her hair pink which always has a pen stuck in her bun.

"Hold on Laurjean, That's not the way to handle this man, I'm thinking. It's a wait and see. It'll be okay Madam Norma said the angels told her so." Laurjean huffs and laughs topping off our cups. Bobby remarks after a big gulp of coffee, "I'm worried, Ken. The guy's a jerk. He would have had me disbarred if he could.

This isn't good. The boxes and activity over at his new store tell me he's got serious merchandise, all from China I bet. I hope Miranda doesn't manage Klaus' store because the woman stalked me for months after I left. I think she even drove into town going slowly several times by my office and my parent's house. I saw her once as I walked down the street and she gave me a piercing, horrible look. It was unsettling.

My angelness comes fast, "Bobby, don't let fear creep in. You know faith always meets fear at the door." I try not to impart too much angel wisdom daily but this time I have to. Justine nods though she has a sad look on her face. And I hurt for her. She's had too much loss and was just rerouting her life when a competitive store opens up and she is faced with her brother's old girlfriend and father's revenge to boot. "My intuition says it's going to be ugly and Mom feels it, too." The server brings the pancakes. Bob, Pam Ellen and Mac walk in for breakfast as well. Can we all join you, yes I know we can," Bob says.

"Dad, Mom, good morning," Bobby rises and hugs them both as does Justine. They greet Mac. I watch Mac look at Justine. He averts his eyes knowing he's staring at her and says hello to us all. As the server moves another table over for them Laurjean comes with her handy coffee pot, pouring everyone a cup. "Hi all, hey Mac and Ken, Stevie wants me to have a little cooking class one day for Billie Jo, Val and Stevie after school when the restaurant is closed. I say how fun."

"Great Laurjean, how nice. You and Donnie are such good cookers as Val says," I laugh."

"It sure is kind of you, Laurjean," Mac smiles. "You are all so welcoming here. I appreciate it and Billie Jo is so happy here."

"Super, the whole fam is here now. You too Mac, you're part of us now. I love little Billie Jo. The kids all play together so well.

Your server will be over again in a jiff." She sashays away and I notice her whole outfit is shocking pink to match her hair even her rhinestone studded pink tennis shoes glitter. "Cool shoes," I say loud enough for all to hear. Donnie comes out of the kitchen wiping his hands on his apron. His halo is above his head but no one sees it but me. Once in a while the halos are visible on us and they sure are pretty to see, iridescent prisms of light. Our bodies glow even though we age with our human experiences. But at night when we fly the glowing is soothing. It soothes little children when they see angels for little one's do see us especially at night. Sometimes adults can see their guardian angels and the glowing but not often. Donnie laughs, "Hey, my favorite people are here. What do you guys want? Sky's the limit today guys. Pancakes?"

Bob pipes up, "Sunshine Pancakes all around?" Bob loves pancakes and eats them most everyday. His waistline shows it.

When chatter is done and plates are served, Bob begins after a huge bite. I can tell Pam Ellen is scared. "This is bullying everyone. I know what Madam Norma said but we are in for a long haul with Klaus. The sign went up just now on his store I'm afraid. It reads, *The Angel and Butterfly Shoppe!* And underneath it says, *NO Angel Parking Here!* He's got angel t-shirts in the window that have butterflies on them but say, *I'm No Angel* and *Got Psychics?*"

Pam Ellen responds, "Not only is he harassing Ken and Justine's store, but mocking the angel sightings as well."

Madam Norma scoots in the door like she psychically knew we'd be here. Miss Marilyn and Tim are by her side. They come over to the table. Laurjean and Donnie come to the table, as do a few customers. Everyone loves Madam Norma and wants to hear what she will say. We move more chairs to the table.

Bob greets them stands up and says in a big voice to the entire restaurant after clinking his glass. "It's time you all should know. A bully has come to Mystic Bay with a Grand Opening tomorrow, same as Jamie Bond's, *Bondo's Bikes*. He's here harassing my children and our town. He will be selling angel and psychic joke gifts. He'll be trying to bring our town's good works and good name down."

A hush runs over the restaurant, and then everyone seems to begin talking at once. This is such an unnecessary mean move and the people of this town are such kind folk. I think with my angelness as hard as I can and say, "But why, Klaus Waxman? His daughter, Miranda is big in the San Francisco social scene Justine says. She's in the paper regularly. She dated some Count recently? I'm sure she's had plenty of men interested especially for her money. Maybe we can talk to him before the opening. I'm willing to do it. I've handled bullies on the football field. He must be a very unhappy soul."

Everyone listens as she begins. Madam Norma puts her tiny hand on mine. "He is a bully and yes, Ken, you can help, but wait til tomorrow. Let me try something first. We all need to be strong and respectful even if the bully isn't. That's how you beat the bully isn't it, Ken? Strength and resolve and being kind to each other and ourselves, right?"

I applaud her wisdom adding, "Madam Norma, you're right. The angels are watching, so let's call on them to help. Each of us ask the angels to help us through."

Bobby stands, "We don't want the media to come back. We've had two media problems in town in the last few years. One when that author, Sam Blakley, asserted Hannah was an angel and another when the angels appeared to the children last summer. Why the media was here again trying to get info on who the kids were and where they lived. They wanted a story at all costs."

Madam Norma weaves her ideas like a delicate lace handkerchief. "Oh yes, he'll pull something with the media. Follow my lead at the Grand Opening Saturday. Bring as many people as you can to Jamie's opening of *Bondo's Bikes*. I'll be there and yes, Ken, we need to ask the angels to be there too." She glances at me for longer than a moment, her blue eyes dancing with the morning light, and then she looks away. I feel my brown angel face in human form flush.

She continues, "The guardian angels will be around everyone. Jamie and I have a plan so be patient. Ken, you interject as you feel necessary that day okay? Now everyone, go back to your tables and enjoy your breakfast. Tomorrow will be quite a red-letter day and I have to get my strength up and eat some pancakes too. More coffee for me, please Laurjean and the delicious blueberry pancakes!"

We all seemed to be obsessed with talking the situation over but I keep thinking about the town, the media and the look on Justine and Pam Ellen's faces. Their intuition can feel the pain that Klaus Waxman's heartlessness will cause before it happens. Bobby's face shows fear, fear for Justine and my angel store, our livelihoods. Bob has usually a more positive attitude as his life as a child was difficult. With two parents addicted to alcohol he found his way through anguish with strong faith and hope. He thought he'd given his own family an almost perfect life in an almost perfect town. Yet, will this be another great lesson for Mystic Bay, standing firmly up to a bullying businessman?

~~~~~~~~~~

It's Saturday. The little lovebirds chirp at our feeder. Val is excited about his sleep over at Justine's tonight and is chatting away how Billie Jo and Heather will be there too, and how Mac is bringing a pizza. It's great Justine has a new friend in Mac. I make Val his favorite scrambled eggs and a smoothie. I have my usual black coffee and banana smoothie and always give a bit of banana to Barty. The angel of a dog loves fruit, the healing food. I do like to eat, as it's a wonderful experience and very satisfying. Val and I eat breakfast talking about the day. Barty eats his dog food when we eat. He's part of the family, of course. As I wash the dishes and Val plays with Barty I glance out the window seeing Justine
~~~~~~~~~~

walking up my path with Walnut trailing behind. She looks pretty dressed for the Grand Opening in jeans and a *Bondo's Bikes* shirt. Jamie gave us all one to wear and Tim paid for everyone who comes in to get one. She's as ready as any of us are to meet Klaus Waxman as Madam Norma predicts that man will come into the store and cause a ruckus of some sort. She has two large bags in each arm. "Morning Justine! What have we here?"

Justine smiles at us. "It's the spaceship comforter set for Val and the butterfly one for Billie Jo. They came last night. I'm so excited for you to put it in your room. Can we go up and make your bed?" We do just that and Val is more than excited. After Val has jumped on the bed with whoops and hollers we take Billie Jo's new comforter over to their place. Mac answers the door with smiling eyes and Billie Jo is thrilled. We all walk up to the little girls room painted yellow, her favorite color. The room looks just perfect for the precious girl. She can hardly believe what's happening. She hugs Justine, then her grandfather, then Val and me. Since it's almost nine we walk across the street through Justine's yard and pass through the alley and her store across the street to *Bondo's Bikes*. A small group has gathered as Jamie opens the door. We note Klaus Waxman standing at his door with a pronounced belly and a black t-shirt that says *I'm No Angel*. Miranda is there too. Her hair is long and brown and her eyes are brown and mad looking. I note she too has a t-shirt same writing but red.

No one is entering Klaus' store. Without greetings, yet I nod to them, we all step into Jamie's store. Bondo is at the back sitting quietly next to Madam Norma. Bobby has walked in behind us and did not acknowledge or look at the Waxman's. The store is getting crowded. Most of the angels including Josh and his wife, Hannah, show up along with many other townsfolk. Last but not least Donnie and Laurjean with her pink hair and Bondo's Bikes t-shirt step in. Jamie quiets everyone down. "Welcome, welcome everyone. Thank you so much for coming to the Grand Opening of *Bondo's Bikes*. Bondo here wishes he could ride a bike too but I got a side car just for him!" Everyone laughs and I look at Bondo. His face is priceless. He almost smiles. "Hey, there's donuts, coffee and juice boxes for the kids. Everyone gets a t-shirt today courtesy of my favorite man, Tim Thayer. And of course I thank my people, Madam Norma, Miss Marilyn and Tim who loaned me the money to start my business. I'd like to thank each of them and wow this is awesome! I also want to thank, Elena, for her support and my darling little Emma Rose. I am one blessed man.

I have a raffle here for a kids' bike and an adult bike. Tickets are five bucks each. Miss Marilyn is collecting for that." As he says his last words the door opens wide and in walks Klaus and Miranda with heads held high and smirks on their faces. "Excuse me," Klaus says in his loud bombastic voice. "You all can come over to my store now to my Grand Opening of *The Angel and Butterfly Shoppe*. I have to tell you we have more than donuts and coffee. We had it catered from San Francisco's *Bon Appetite!* Everyone gets an *I'm No Angel* t-shirt." Quiet isn't the word. Silence and stares permeate the room. Finally, Madam Norma states, "Excuse me, sir, hello, everyone knows me in town, I'm Madam Norma. This is Jamie Bond. Mr. Bond's Grand Opening is today and we notice so is yours. However, we have children here with us today and so we must be examples for those children and be polite don't you think?" Not waiting for an answer she continues, "Please go along now and perhaps you will have some interest in your new store. Maybe some customers have already arrived." She smiles behind calculating eyes. The seven of us take deep breaths, which make our bodies appear larger than they are. No one notices except Klaus and Miranda.

"This is ridiculous!" Klaus laughs. Madam Norma turns to Jamie and they start talking, ignoring Klaus and his daughter as if they are invisible. Then Klaus does something really foolish. He raises his voice again. "Just see you old whatever- your -name -is what I can do to this town! Watch and see at ten o'clock what will be happening. Just you wait!" The seven us start to head for the door single file walking toward him. The surprised look on Klaus and Miranda's face is notable as our strength only they can see is massive walking in silent reverie. They leave quickly and the angel wind shuts the door. "There," says the brilliant Madam Norma, "let the party begin again." Jamie looks relieved and so am I, but what is Klaus talking about? I think I know what's going to happen.

Chapter 5

Faith Meets Fear

At ten some folks are leaving. We spot Dan Pica of the *San Francisco Chronicle* interviewing Klaus. His daughter must be inside. Justine and Mac take Billie Jo's hands walking her quickly across the street to *The Painted Butterfly*. I follow with Val and head for the store. I look back to see Bobby come up to Klaus saying something. With my angel ear I can hear clearly what is said. Klaus Waxman pushes Bobby. Bobby pushes him back. Dan Pica tries talking to both. I turn back to usher Val in.

"What's happening Dad?" Val senses the tension; he's innocent in some ways yet what he says next gives me a vision into his old world with his mother. "Is someone going to hit somebody?" Billie Jo looks scared also. Angie walks in from my store. "What's happening?"

"Reporters are here and Mr. Waxman is not being polite and is starting, uh, well, an argument, Angie. He really needs help. It's sad he has to act that way but everything will work out." Mac says, "Justine, do you want to go back to our house? Your store doesn't open until eleven."

"No, thanks Mac. I'm going to stay right here and wait for Bobby and my parents." She obviously didn't see the altercation. Maybe she sensed it. Mac offers to take Val with him, and let Barty out. "I want to see that fort you're building, Val. We can have a picnic." I tell them I'll be there shortly. They walk out the door and Bobby walks in and plunks down on the flowered sofa. Pam Ellen and Bob walk in too. Justine goes to him. "What happened?"

"Klaus was telling Dan Pica that the whole town is lying, that there weren't really angel sightings last year. He said that he put his store here to prove it. He says all we want is money from tourists and there's a horrible lawyer and family in town who's made up this whole story. He pointed directly at me. I walked up to him and said, "Calm down, this is nuts!" He pushed me and I pushed him back. Gabe and Donnie rushed up and called the police. I can't believe this is happening. I can't believe this is all over me breaking up with Miranda and we weren't even a couple! My God I never should have pushed him back."

"You're human, Bobby, a natural reaction."

Justine's look is painful. Bob and Pam Ellen talk candidly about the incident. Pam Ellen says, "Klaus started it and we noticed Miranda at the window looking triumphant." Pam Ellen is visibly shaken. "Pushing and shoving has never happened in Mystic Bay."

"I know Mom, " Bobby is distressed. "I feel awful."

I think fast. "Walk over right now and apologize, Bobby, even though you didn't start it."

"Okay. I just don't think it will do any good."

"Just wait one minute before you go over there." I leave, crossing the street again, figuring out what the angels can do. I pass Donnie, who is the former police chief, walking over to *The Painted Butterfly*. I tell him what I'm thinking and he agrees. We say our goodbyes and how we are looking forward to flying tonight from my roof. We'll all discuss the situation then.

The reporter remains at Klaus' store. Madam Norma is outside in her motorized chair with pink ribbons decorating the sides and has witnessed it all. Chief Jim Nero is talking to Klaus. Jamie Bond is by Madam Norma's side ready to deck Klaus at a moments notice but Madam Norma is holding his hand. Bondo is anxiously standing by Madam Norma's scooter guarding her.

Madam Norma puts up her hand. "Could I say something here, Chief?" Without waiting for the Chief's approval she goes on. "Mr. Klaus, I have a feeling your emotions got the better of you. Perhaps you were upset that no one was appreciative of your coming into Bondo's Bikes. I get you, I really do. Chief Nero, I'm sure Mr. Klaus is sorry for starting a fight with Mr. Bobby, aren't you Mr. Klaus?"

"My name is Waxman not Klaus. That's my first name!"

"Oh yes, I forgot, I'm a very old lady, Mr. Klaus, very old." Madam Norma is so wise. "Listen, come see me Mr. Klaus anytime to talk. I'm the oldest lady and psychic in this town. I live on Moon Road and was born and raised here. My late husband was the only lawyer for years here. Then Bobby moved back to practice and we were all thrilled. I have a lot to say to you if you'll come see me for a cup of tea. Goodbye then. Come, Jamie, you still have a grand Grand Opening and *Bondo's Bikes* to sell." She scoots off next door with her purple wisdom aura surrounding her and her white hair glittering like a feathery halo. Jamie walks with her though he looks back at Klaus giving him a dirty look. Bondo looks back too.

I walk up to Chief Nero and stand very close to Klaus, invading his space." How can I help?" I look at Klaus then. "Mr. Waxman, I'm Ken Leighton, the owner of *Heaven Can't Wait*, the angel store across the street. Yes, you have a right to free speech, but I'm sure you can find other ways that are more helpful to your store, sir." I grow taller glowing which I make sure only he can see. Klaus looks at me perplexed and wide-eyed. I've made an impact. He can't understand why but he's uneasy yet in awe around me. For as I told Bobby, faith always meets fear at the door.

"I have a right to free speech and say anything I want. I've got a business now. This town lies. No angels have been here and the psychics are fake, too." Chief Nero tries to explain that if Bobby wants he can file charges as Klaus started the fight.

Klaus Waxman suddenly looks at me. "You're the former coach

of the San Francisco Shakers!"

"Yes, Mr. Waxman, I am." I stand firm towering over him; my presence is enormous, my glowing blinding him.

He backs up a few spaces, "I never liked that team." He waits for me to react for a moment, fists up in the air, yet I stand and look at him, growing taller by the second. Klaus puts his hands over his eyes as if the glowing hurts and turns his head back saying to Chief Nero, "I was intimidated by Bobby Delaney and I'm a powerful San Francisco attorney. You both are wrong. You can't charge me with anything. But I could charge him. Just watch me!" He huffs; turning back to his store, but Bobby walks up. "Klaus, I'm sorry I pushed you. I hope you'll accept my apology." Bobby sticks out his hand.

"You've got to be kidding, you liar. You broke my Miranda's heart. I'm going to make you really sorry!" As he leaves Chief of Police big and tall Jim Nero says firmly, "That's a threat and I will document it." Klaus shrugs his shoulders and walks back into his store. The former motionless crowd starts leaving but a few curious tourists walk into his store. Dan Pica is a good guy but he has a story to write. Most folks inquisitive to see the store's contents are the summer tourists who frequent our town. Chief Nero writes on a pad saying goodbye to me but adds, "Let's talk, Bobby." He shakes his head and he and Bobby walk back across the street. The bully has met his match in Madam Norma and me, the seventh angel. I stop in my tracks at sidewalks edge realizing Val called me Dad'! It's a new beginning for Val and me…. a new trust.

Chapter 6

The Challenge

We're up on my roof. All seven of us this time thanks to Justine's babysitting Heather and Val. It's midnight and we are about to take off on wings of angels. Justine, Val and Heather are sleeping. Mac brought pizza over and all the kids played happily she texted me. We angels went out for dinner at *The Pelican Wharf* in San Francisco as a ruse for our pretend meeting but of course couldn't discuss angel business of Mystic Bay for fear someone would hear. We did discuss the Bay Area Sports Program and our needs and expectations for the future. A few customers recognized July and she was polite and signed autographs. Someone recognized me and wanted to talk football. As we drove home in Josh's seven-passenger van we spoke of Klaus Waxman and the incident. We decided the people in town would stand firm as they have in the past. The challenge will be overcome but lessons will be learned on handling negative people like Klaus. Good comes out of the bad and we angels will be there. I tell them of my phone call with Madam Norma. She and I have a plan for what hopefully will bring some help. But now as the clock strikes twelve midnight it's our turn.

We fly in geese formation, Gabe at the head and Taylor and me at the rear. Gliding above the harbor again and out to the sea to feel the mist as always we come back flying just above the rooftops of the houses of our little town. Main Street is our favorite for it is long and lit all night. This peacefulness is calming to angels and humans alike. The rare dog out for a stroll with his or her human companion looks up at our presence. Lone cats sleeping on windowsills or back porches look up with disinterest. Hannah, Gabe's daughter, Josh's wife, is at their bedroom window and waves remembering her nights flying with her father and even now she flies occasionally with her Josh. We fly to the east to the ranches and hills over sleeping farm animals oblivious to our passing as we swoosh down. We know with our angelness someone very nearby is praying for angel help at this very moment. We hear praying coming from Doc Lindley's red barn. He's tending one of the many Fallow deer he rescued. She's giving birth and it's becoming difficult we see as we set softly down. The old doctor mentored vet and angel Josh. His strength is not what it used to be and he needs help. We angels are invisible to old Doc. But Doc Josh and Taylor are next to him now placing their strong hands on his arms giving him the strength needed. Doc Lindley looks back to see if someone is standing there because he's feeling strong helping hands on his forearms. Once the fawn is safely out on the hay we stay a moment. He looks at the doe and fawn in wonder. We have formed a circle of love around him and he starts to cry quietly. He looks around. "Whoever you are, I can't see you, but I know you are here. Are you the angels that come to Mystic Bay? If you are, I thank you." He turns back to the deer, wiping his eyes with his sleeve.

Donnie smiles at us, nods and instantly we are up and away from the ranch. I watch the others fly in formation before me. Each of their wings has color of it's own; shine with glittering texture. As different as snowflakes or the planets and stars of the universe so are the wings of angels. Our glowing kindness is the beacon for us all to follow. Over the tops of the farms and ranches we fly back into town happy to help our friend for one night. As we head back to our prospective homes waving a goodnight to each other, I hear with my angel's ear as I pass by his parent's house, Bobby asking God and the angels for help. The lights are on in his bedroom so I stand by him for a moment. I send an angel-calming wind of love and kindness to him with my outstretched hand. I see his shoulders relax. I see him sit back on his bed, turn off the light and lie down again on his soft pillow. His eyes close and I sprinkle a bit of angel sleeping dust and he is in peaceful slumber.

I fly instantly to look at Val and Billy Jo sleeping in the twin beds of Liz' room. Heather is in a little crib. Justine has put a cot in the room and is sleeping peacefully. No need to sprinkle angel dust. Now I'm home in an instant to find Barty waiting for me in my room. When I found him that rainy night years ago in an alley in San Francisco, I swept the young pup in my arms and we flew toward home. He nestled in my arms and the bond was formed. He does his three curls by my bed and his eyes close knowing his angel human is home. Before Val came, Barty would sleep by my bed each night for years. Now he knows he's got a job to protect and love a little boy whose sleep is improving, yet there is still restlessness. I look out the window at the night fog clearing. The bright lovely moon shines on the homes on my street. "What a ride, Barty," I say to my wonder dog. "There's a challenge in town and somehow we angels will help our flock. Goodnight, my faithful friend, goodnight!"

Chapter 7

Here She Comes Again!

It's been a tense week in Mystic Bay. The residents are upset at the discord Klaus Waxman's store and angel rants are causing. Laurjean especially is unnerved. She has prepared a petition and asks everyone that comes in *The Next Door Café* to sign it. The petition says, "With respect we request only peace and consideration by the business owners of Mystic Bay." So far many have signed, but the Mayor says it is just a request and wouldn't hold up in a court of law so it's best to leave it alone. Madam Norma and I have written a request for an informal meeting with Klaus and Miranda via mail and a note placed through the slot in the store's front door. We offered to meet at Madam Norma's home on Moon Road, but so far there has been no response.

Bobby is working in his office and venturing home late at night to his parents when he knows Miranda and her father have left for home in San Francisco. However, everyone notices how Miranda sashays up and down the street a few times a day stopping outside the door that leads to his upstairs office. She hasn't come in *The Painted Butterfly* as yet but Justine predicts she will. Justine will call upon one of us to come over when it happens. So as some tourists are seen wearing the dreaded *I'm No Angel* and *Got Psychics* t-shirts from Klaus' store, life goes on.

The kids are off to school; Bobby joins Mac and me for coffee at Justine's store. The smell of coffee is something I've grown to love. We sip our coffees and sit around the table with me on the couch before opening our business. Our topic this morning turns to Val and Billie Jo. "I have an announcement," Justine says with a twinkle in her eye. "When I was babysitting Val and Billie Jo on Sunday they both wanted to paint butterflies and so I got all my paints out and set up everything on the table for us to paint. I was instructing them on simple brush strokes, my hand on Billie Jo's when a wonderful thing happened! It's been over a year since I painted but I just took the brush and began painting a butterfly on the paper with my hand over hers. It was just like I'd never stopped painting! My mother will be thrilled now. So, it's my turn to get cracking and put this yellow butterfly in the window." She turns picking up her latest painting, a yellow Monarch on a black background. Every week a different butterfly painting and objects all butterfly grace the large storefront window. Usually the painting is sold in a week. Pam Ellen has prayed the angels would help Justine paint again and it's finally happened.

"That's great, Sis," Bobby exclaims hugging her. I also congratulate her, as does Mac. It's so good to see her smile stay longer then a moment on her sweet face. Smiles are staying longer on Billie Jo and Val's faces too. This makes my heart sing.

Justine admits, "The children are so dear. It's really a gift to have them in my world and caring for them has changed my focus. I miss Mike and Liz, but I still have a life, a purpose. I'm trying to look forward, not back. But there's more. I found this children's book I wrote for Mike and Liz when they were young. I have a copyright but never published. Although my book was just for us I made two copies one for each of you." She hands us both manila envelopes. "It's called *God's Shoulder.* It seemed to comfort the kids when they were Val and Billie Jo's age. I hope they'll like it."

"Thank you so much, Justine. How wonderful!" Mac smiles at her and I concur with, "Yes thank you. I can't wait to read it with Val!" The conversation quiets as we hear a commotion outside on the street. We go over to look out the window. There we see what's happening and walk out the door. There in front of *The Angel and*

Butterfly Shoppe is a TV station truck and the unwelcome reporter, Tiffany Gould. A few years ago this infuriating reporter in her micro mini skirt caused the whole town problems. When author, Sam Blakley, wrote his novel, *My California Angel,* insinuating a real angel lived in California and the word spread he was outing Gabe's daughter Hannah; the story went viral. Hannah kept the secret safe with July North's brilliant idea of hosting a TV show in Town Square.

Her idea centered on exposing Sam Blakley as a would-be liar. What nobody, especially Sam Blakley realized was there was truth in what he wrote. As Sam plagiarized all of Hannah's creative writing papers she wrote in his class depicting flybys with her angel dad, Sam was writing the truth. Sam never realized Gabe was an angel, he thought Hannah was writing fiction. Sam just wanted her back and didn't understand Hannah is actually half angel and she was writing beloved memories as her creative writing stories for his class. When Hannah broke up with Sam, he put her stories to pen and established them as part of the story in his novel. But good prevailed and even though the realities of his assertions were technically true, his ultimate goal was to mess with Hannah's mind and win her back.

We all learned a lot from this event a few years back. Hannah went on to write her own book called *The Town With the Angel Vibe* thanking the town for their support of friendship during the most difficult time. No one would talk to the media while they were in town. It was as if everyone shut down. The town will ultimately do the same now.

After Sam left the thought of angels inspired the town with hope and thanksgiving. A loving angelic spirit spread through the town. Townsfolk started fervently rescuing animals; volunteering to help others less fortunate and some even fostered and adopted children. Calculating Tiffany Gould didn't show her face when July North hosted another TV Show after the angels appeared to the children last year. Tiffany must have known it must be a true miracle and she stayed away. But now that there is some evidence of negativity toward the town, her antennae are up and ready for action. Her poor common sense seems revenge inspired for her humiliation and firing from her network. Now she works for local TV station in San Francisco, KFWW. I can tell she's raring to get the story like a rodeo steer wants out of the shoot.

"Oh no," Justine says. "Not her again."

Angie and Ricky join us, as the stores don't open for fifteen minutes. "What's going on?" Ricky is worried, as already our sales have plummeted since Klaus' store opened. I have told him not to worry. This will be short lived although how short lived is only a psychics guess.

Sassy Laurjean practically runs up the street waving her hand at Tiffany Gould. Laurjean, always a colorful dresser, wears a lime green pantsuit, lime green platforms and pop-it beads necklace. "Go home, little Miss Tiffany! This town is to be peaceful and I for one won't have my youngest son grow up with your type of bullying." Tiffany snubs her nose and turns away knocking on Klaus's door. Laurjean's pink hair and lime green outfit look absolutely right for the occasion. I, the biggest man in town, walk across the street wanting to stand before her. I send her a flashback from the past of the day she stormed into Hannah and Gabe's store.

Klaus comes out of *The Angel and Butterfly Shoppe's* front door and I decide to grow taller and glow as I step over the curb, "What's this all about Mr. Waxman? And hello Miss, I'm Ken Leighton, the former coach of the San Francisco Shakers!" Tiffany looks at me unimpressed and pretending not to hear she asks Klaus, "Hello, Mr. Waxman, tell me in your own words what you think is going on here in Mystic Bay?"

Her small cameraman is having trouble with his camera.

"Fix it, you fool," Tiffany says to the cameraman. But Klaus can't wait, shooting me a dirty look replying as his stomach expands, " I'm here in Mystic Bay to tell the world there were no angel sightings here, only a big marketing scheme. The Delaney family is at the heart of this mockery. They own that butterfly store across the street and their son's a no good attorney who broke my daughter's heart. He used to work for me. No one is psychic, believe you me, because it's all a souped up game to get people here to buy the angel, butterfly and psychic stuff." He grunts happy with his answer.

Tiffany almost squeals with delight, " Wow, this is big news. So the town is pretending to be psychic, you think, and lying by telling the world that angels appeared to little kids?"

"It's very sad," reports Klaus. "And I for one am standing tall against all of them!" The cameraman gets his camera to work amazingly at the exact moment Laurjean pipes up in Laurjean fashion, "Listen you two, ANGELS did appear to little children. It WAS a miracle and we all won't let you bring your negativity here to our serene town! We won't take the abuse. This is bullying!"

The camera stops working as Klaus laughs, "What you gonna do about it, you green centipede. I'm so glad you came, Miss Gould. Come inside and meet my lovely daughter. You two are so pretty like sisters, long hair and all." They start to walk in but I stop them in a whispering angel voice that only Tiffany can hear. " Miss Gould, perhaps you should rethink your decision to toy with the town again. Beautiful things are happening here in Mystic Bay. People are adopting children, rescuing animals, starting programs for disadvantaged youth. The angel paintings and recording were taken on tour around the world and now they are housed in the free museum in Riverton. Everyone who goes there loves the music and the artwork inspired by the angels. It would be wonderful if you'd report on these topics. You know it in your soul. Remember you were angered for the loss of your job a few years back when you reported on Sam Blakely's book. It was discovered he was plagiarizing Hannah's writings. That did not serve you well, Tiffany." Tiffany is mesmerized by my voice. She sways a little and I hold her arm. I send angel wind and another sudden flashback of the day she stormed into Hannah's store demanding to know if Hannah was a real angel. Tiffany is in instant tears. Her mascara goops and forms a little black smudge under her eyes. She runs her hands through her bleach blond hair and her fingers get caught in a snarl. "Who are you?" Her cameraman stares at me but couldn't hear what I said as his camera starts to roll.

"Ken Leighton, I own *Heaven Can't Wait* angel store across the street." Tiffany continues to stare at me but Klaus takes her arm. "Don't listen to whatever he said to you dear, please come into my store." They walk into Klaus's store, Tiffany looking back at me. I know I've made an impact. She could see my glowing, knowing in her heart I was right. She remembered in amazing detail the day she bullied Hannah. She also remembered the shame when she lost her big job and her large salary and she walked humiliated pass the desks of the others in the office with her box of things from her desk, She remembers how hard it was to get a job again. But Sam Blakely, the author, who she dated for a while got her an interview with the station KFWW and she persuaded them to give her a try.

I nod at Tiffany's guardian angel standing by. He let's me know he's tried hard to guide her but so far nothing is working, Her life's goal is materialism and revenge so similar to Miranda Waxman's. Her reaction gave him hope he communicates to me. Then he is gone in a flash of light.

A few tourists go inside the store after them and Laurjean and I stand alone. "I couldn't hear you, Ken. You know I couldn't but thank you! Tiffany was a-listening big time. You are such a sweet angelic soul!" She winks for, of course, she's Angel Donnie's wife and knows our secret. She knows I can talk to someone and they are the only ones who can hear me. "I doubt you made a dent in her mind, if you don't mind me telling you. I just think she was mesmerized by your voice, your size, your glow! I'm frustrated, Ken. How can I help?"

"Laurjean, you just keep being the wonderful you we all love, the vigilante and cheerleader for the town. Donnie and I and the others will keep putting out angel wind and ideas to the people involved. There is free will; of course, we all have it even us angels. But heaven only knows only time will tell, yet, I'm pretty hopeful today! "

"I hope you're right, Big Ken, I hope you're right. Hey, want to come for breakfast? It's on me."

"Yes, I will. But first I've got to go back over to see Bobby and Justine." I don't tell her my concern for the town and media exposure again. This will be the third time we have been in the news in five years. I walk back to *The Painted Butterfly* as the Bell Tower strikes nine and Justine, Mac and Bobby are still looking out the door. I wave to Angie and Ricky as they walk back to my store. I will tell them I tried to talk to her about the angel sightings but nothing more. Our angel workings are to be a secret just like our presence. It's always been this way and it always will be.

Through the Eyes of Children

Bobby, Justine, her parents, Mac and I are gathered around Justine's TV. We watch knowing the kids are outside playing in the sunshine with the dogs and with their ingenious imagination. Tiffany's TV report is on the six o'clock news. It begins, "I'm here in Mystic Bay, California inside the new store, *The Angels and Butterfly Shoppe* with shop owner, Klaus Waxman. He's well known as partner in San Francisco's prestigious law firm Waxman and Faille. Mr. Waxman, why did you open *The Angel and Butterfly Shoppe* here? There is a butterfly shop across the street and an angel store too?" Klaus Waxman is not photogenic. He's a beast of a man with a curmudgeon look on his face. "I am so sick and tired of a town like this pretending to be pious about those angel sightings? Phooey! It's all a mockery, I tell you." Klaus frowns. "They just want money! Believe me no kids saw angels, Miss Gould!"

"But many believe it to be true, Mr. Waxman."

"It's falderal, I tell you!" Turning he shouts, "Ralph! Hold up the t-shirts I'm selling. Look at these!"

Klaus' sales associate holds up the t-shirts that read, *I'm NO Angel* and *Got Psychics*.

"I don't believe people are psychic. It's all pretend like fairyland!" Klaus' brow beads with sweat and I notice his eyes look quite angry. I also notice his guardian angel materialize for a moment. No one else sees him of course. The angel shakes his head in disappointment. He transmits to all the other angels near through silence, "He's so much to learn. His learning may have to happen in Heaven's Realm." Then the brilliantly colored angels' wings are gone. I sigh.

We are momentarily silent, for I didn't tell them too much about Laurjean's interview although I witnessed it. I was at Laurjean's having a delicious breakfast and Tiffany kept looking at me the whole time. I just sat there consuming Sunshine Pancakes. They all were doubtful when I told them but they now see it with their own eyes. The next segment of the interview is Tiffany Gould at *The Next Door Café* interviewing Laurjean. Donnie stays out of the limelight as we all seven must. "I'm here with Mrs. Laurjean Whitefeather, owner of *The Next Door Café* here in Mystic Bay. I am aware you have a petition going. Let me read it here." She reads it with emotion surprisingly. "So tell us what your thoughts are now that you heard Mr. Waxman's viewpoint."

"Call me Laurjean please and land sakes, this town had miracles happen, dearie. Two of the children must remain anonymous. But Benny Chen is the child who angels taught a beautiful song. He played it on the piano for the world to have in its keeping. Why wonderful things are happening here, Miss Gould. We have *The Angel Museum* in Riverton where the artwork the angels inspired a child to paint is displayed and the angel's song is played in earphones for all to hear. The museum is free to all and the angel artwork and the beautiful music have toured around the world. There are psychics in this town, too, and I know many of them. They're just a part of us. Typical people going about their lives like all of us. We don't want to be attacked by someone who wants revenge hurting our picturesque peaceful little town by the sea. Didn't you see the July North Show on the sightings? "

Tiffany shakes her blond head. "Maybe you should watch it. Our children are watching us, Tiffany. They're watching how we handle this bully-like-behavior."

"You call this bullying, Laurjean. Do you think it is?"

"Let me read this." Laurjean reads from a piece of paper. "From Webster's Dictionary. A Bully is a person who is 'a blustering, browbeating person: especially: one who is habitually cruel, insulting or threatening to others who are weaker, smaller, or in some way vulnerable.' I will not judge anyone, I'm just saying, Tiffany, what a lot of us are feeling." The customers in the restaurant start applauding. Tiffany is back on camera. She looks at the camera with liquid eyes where tears are forming. "Well, there you have it, two very different views from two business owners. Reporting live for KFWW from Mystic Bay, I'm Tiffany Gould."

Everyone is silent but Mac says, "I wasn't here then but I think the reporter did try to get both viewpoints. What do you all think?" As they discuss the report, I feel good. Giving Tiffany an exact flashback made all the difference. She might not have thought to interview anyone else but remembered Laurjean and knew that her last interviews were so negative and how she verbally attacked Hannah. She was fairer this time. Everyone agrees amazed at just how fair an interview it was. "She's making a change," notes Justine. "Her demeanor was different. Something happened to her. Something made her think. Did you say something to her, Ken?"

Anticipating this, "Yes, I told her to remember how last time she was here during the *My California Angel* book debacle, she lost her job over the scathing brutal way she went after Hannah. She was relentless. I didn't use those words. I only reminded her how she lost her important network job over it. Maybe she thought about it."

"Well done, Ken," says Bob. Bobby agrees and Pam Ellen says, "I pick up Tiffany had some type of epiphany! Tiffany's epiphany, get it?" We all laugh at that. "She didn't interview Miranda. Bobby, you're quiet. What is your take?"

"I just can't believe how far Klaus has taken his anger in spending the money and time to rent a building, the effort it took to make t-shirts and sell angel and butterfly trinkets, to go to all this trouble to upset me and my family and the town? And Miranda is acting so weird walking up and down the streets of town, going into shops, and saying nothing. People tell me she's just buying things. She stands outside The Painted Butterfly and my office. It's weird, I tell you!"

Bob remarks, "Yes, son. I actually feel sorry for Miranda because her father has spoiled her so much. That's what Pam Ellen and Justine think, don't you?"

"Yes, dear," remarks Pam Ellen. " I would guess Miranda had no parameters, no rules of any kind ever. Maybe it's because her mother died? Bobby you said she gets an allowance, cars and a condo and pays nothing. No job, no volunteering, and no purpose. She just spends and vacations. That can't be a good life for anyone!"

"She was so different from me," Bobby says. "I can't get why she would let her father do this. I really don't!"

"Revenge does things to people," Mac remarks. "She's not thinking how she must look to others, the selfishness."

Bobby continues, "But it's working, isn't it? He's on the six o'clock news. He may get national press. It's hurting the town's spirit; it's made everyone uneasy. It's taking away the rush of happiness and thanksgiving."

"It's not going to work," predicts Justine. "I feel it, don't you Mom?" Pam Ellen nods her lovely expression so like her daughter's. "We better ask the angels for a little more help. They might want to try angel visions in another town!"

I decide to extend my hand like I'm stretching but in reality I send a few butterflies into the backyard garden to the kids and dogs.

As we're setting the table getting ready for the pizza to be delivered, Billie Jo, Val and the dogs run in the house. The kids are almost breathless. "Dad, Dad, guess what? A butterfly landed on

Walnut's nose? We want to paint butterflies on paintings of dogs noses and put them in the store window!" Billie Jo adds enthusiastically, "And butterflies on cats, too and all kinds of animals, like cows!" All the adults look at each other in awe and joy at what has just happened. The innocent thoughts of children and the sending of butterflies at this moment changed everything. I envision *The Painted Butterfly's* window with the paintings. Everyone who admires the store will love them. "How about painting butterflies on angels wings for your store, Ken?" Justine has a lovely idea!

"Splendid," I say clapping my hands as a twinkling glows in my angel eyes…

Chapter 9

God's Shoulder by Justine Greer

I sit on Val's bed. We do this every night to read a story. This time he will be able to read most of Justine's book to me.

Dad," he says looking up at me with big brown eyes. "Why did Justine give me this book? Why does Justine like me?"

My eyes tear a bit when answering, "You are a good boy, Val and we are lucky to have a nice boy like you in our lives. Justine wrote this book for Mike and Liz when they were your age to show them how much she loved them. Wait til we read it together then we will talk about it. Now you read first and I'll help with the words you don't know. Okay?"

Barty snores softly on his bed and Val and I laugh at that. The bedside lamp catches a soft glow as we open the hand written book, *"God's Shoulder"* The photo on the front is of Penny, their old dog that passed away a few years ago, and their cat named Kitty. Val snuggles down, ready for our reading adventure, a book to treasure and to love.

God's Shoulder

Penny yawned.

Time for bed, the dog thought.

Off she trotted towards the twin's bedroom.

She stopped in the doorway.

Mom was singing a lullaby to the twins, Mike and Liz.

Oh, Singing makes me sleepy thought Penny.

Mom said, "Remember at night when you are saying your prayers you can lie on your pillow and pretend it's God's shoulder. He can comfort you when you are sad, mad or just need to think or pray.

When I was little I would pretend my pillow was God's shoulder. I still do sometimes.

Goodnight, Sweet dreams," Mom whispered as she kissed each one goodnight.

Penny had listened very carefully.

God's shoulder sounds nice, she thought.

She jumped up on the bed and snuggled next to Mike.

He was saying his prayers.

Penny gave a little sigh as she placed her head on Mike's pillow.

Kitty who had been curled at Liz's feet was pretending not to listen.

Me too, she purred.

So Kitty pranced to the pillow and put her head right next to sweet, sleeping Liz.

"Dad, " I like this God's Shoulder book!

"I'm so glad. We will have to thank Justine tomorrow. Sweet dreams, my son."

Chapter 10

The Tale of Two Shops

Pam Ellen has been mostly minding the store. Justine has set up an easel. All who come in the shop love watching her paint the butterflies on the noses of dogs, cats and cows. Justine even painted a white angel with rainbow wings with a butterfly on her shoulder. We put that one in the *Heaven Can't Wait* window and Angie and Ricky say it sold in one afternoon! Business has picked up and Justine hopes angel paintings will sell like the pancakes at *The Next Door Café*. Laurjean and Donnie placed one in their restaurant window too. People stop and stare at the windows all day. Justine has renewed purpose.

All has calmed down this week as far as Klaus Waxman goes. He's lying low we guess. Mac is bringing home a rescued white poodle mix today to surprise Billie Jo for her birthday. Mac has everything set. We will all be at the picnic on hand this evening.

Our Saturday rooftop fly was wondrous and the misty rain was a benefit. We soared above the low clouds then high again enough to see a myriad of stars. It took our angel breath away. The moon was high and our angel hearts felt good. Our only topic was how to encourage Klaus to leave town. We angels, of course, can't do it ourselves; the townsfolk are slowly inching towards strength in numbers by getting on with their lives. It's not the topic of conversation this week. They're not caving in to Klaus' foolishness.

We're having our morning coffee at Justine's store. Mac tells us, "It will be such a amazing day for Billie Jo today when she comes home from school. Pam Ellen and Bob will keep the dog at their house till after we've started the picnic. Gabe is bringing his pet squirrel, Bubbles, to entertain the kids with his tricks. Before we have the picnic supper, Pam Ellen will walk in with the dog. I'm so excited for her."

Justine remarks, "Oh, so wonderful. She's totally blossomed being with you. She loves school and her new friends. You have done an awesome job."

"Thank you both! You and Ken have helped me so much!"

I interject. "It's been such a wonderful few months. The surprise for Val today is January is bringing his cousin, Spencer, to the party. The adoption has gone through. July will be there also with Heather and it will be a great birthday party for her."

"Miranda will walk over in a moment," says Justine. She looks out the window as Miranda walks across the street and up to the store and proceeds to stare in the window. Miranda dressed for a party in a cocktail dress and hair all messy looks as if she's been up all night. She has an angry look on her face. Justine waves. Turning to Bobby Justine says, "Maybe you should talk to her, Bobby." Bobby gets up and starts to walk upstairs to his office saying, "No, I'm not going to encourage her behavior." Justine moves to the door and opens it. Bobby stops and turns around. Justine says kindly, "Miranda."

Miranda pushes by her, "Bobby, I need to talk to you." She gives us all dirty looks and shouts; "I don't respect you for ignoring me. I know you've blocked me from your phone and email. My dad opened a business here and you people have been horrible to us in your stupid town. You'll be sorry!" Miranda's childish behavior is surprising. She's acting like a spoiled teenager. I'm guessing she's in her early thirties.

I walk up to her. My glowing size gives Miranda pause. "And you are?"

"I'm Ken Leighton. I own the shop next door." My glowing

strength is scaring her.

" Bobby," she almost screams. "I'm going to sue you for making me look pathetic in front of my friends. Everyone's asking me about you. No one has ever broken up with me. I'm going on social media. You haven't heard the last of it."

"Miranda, I'm sorry if I've hurt you. I wish you happiness and love," is all Bobby says. He turns to go up the stairs. "You have ruined my reputation. I found someone else!" She actually sticks out her tongue but Bobby walks up the stairs ignoring her.

Justine says, "Goodbye Miranda, we do really wish you the best." She stands at the door, holding it open and Miranda huffs out. Justine closes the door but we can see through the glass as Miranda turns on her heel crossing the street with stilettos clicking. We see her get into her silver new Mercedes convertible. We see her speed away honking the horn in anger at the store, turning her livid face our way and unfortunately for me, I can hear her expletives. It's like a scene from a bad movie.

Klaus comes out of his store and watches her go. He says something to his sales' associate, gets into his fancy black Mercedes sedan and speeds away toward his spoiled daughter. Maybe it'll be over soon, I'm thinking. Although something tells me we have a way to go with this.

Everyone is speechless but me, "You two were nice to her and took the high road."

"It's sad," says Mac. " They both need help."

We all agree, but it's time to open our stores. I walk over to my store saying goodbye to all. I stop at the front store window and my angel heart skips a beat. Justine has painted a beautiful angel in a flowing pink gown with dark hair piled on her head with olive skin and dark eyes. She has a purple butterfly on her shoulder. What's astounded me is Justine has painted July's face on the angel! Does she know July's an angel? She can't know. She's psychic for sure but I can't believe what I'm seeing. I walk back into *The Painted Butterfly* and Justine is helping a customer. She tells me to wait a moment. When the customer is busy looking at a butterfly tea cup set she inquires, "What is it Ken, you look distraught?"

"No, not distraught, dear, not at all. I just saw your newest angel butterfly painting. She has July's face!"

"Oh yes, isn't it fun, Ken? I'm going to put all the friends faces I admire in angel paintings. If they want it, I'll give it to them for they are truly the angels on earth. " I laugh albeit, nervously. "What a great idea! Are you going to make me an angel dear?" The irony of what I've said surprises even me.

"Why yes, you're next! I'm going to put sheen to your skin like Taylor's, and I'll paint him too. People need to know angels come in all sizes, colors and shapes. I'm even going to make angel dogs like Barty and Walnut with butterflies on their noses. I'm on a roll with this!"

"Wow,"I hug her. "You are so creative!"

"I don't know about that, I just know I feel lucky the kids came up with the idea. Look, I'm putting their own paintings in the window." The customer asks her a question and I say goodbye. Walking back to my store I feel hopeful. Today is going to be a great day for my family. Spencer is coming for Val; Billie Jo will finally get her dog. Yes, a wonderful day it is.

<center>~~~~~~~~~</center>

To say the birthday picnic was a success is an understatement. Val cried when he saw Spencer. They could not stop holding on to each other and talking. Everyone had tears in their eyes. Bubbles the squirrel was a roaring success, jumping from Gabe's shoulder to the picnic table where the kids tossed peanuts to him. He delighted us all by catching each one perfectly, then chattering and begging with arms out to the next child. Gabe took Bubbles home and we ate sandwiches and potato salad under the sunny California sky. The trees were swaying in the breeze. Billie Jo was all smiles and then Pam Ellen strolled in the yard with the white fluffy young dog in hand. Billie Jo stood and was motionless for a moment. Her pure joy should have been captured in a photo but I will remember it for all my existence. Billie Jo ran to the dog then stopped short a few paces from Pam Ellen. She outstretched her hands. She remained still as Pam Ellen placed the little dog in her arms. She immediately hugged her as Mac made sure he'd picked the gentlest dog he could find. Billie Jo named her Sadie. I looked up at the faces of both my angel friends and human friends and their looks filled with love and kindness. Thanksgiving enveloped me. I couldn't help it. I stretched my arm out for a moment and butterflies from the garden seemed to congregate and flutter through the crowd. No one noticed my connection to the butterflies. They never do.

Chapter 11

Renewal

After our happy day yesterday it is a cooler than normal today as thunderclouds rolled in from the sea and hopes for much needed California rain. We are just ending our coffee klatch when Klaus walks out of his store and people start to gather as he shouts. We all walk out the front door to see what's brewing now. Shops are opening and storeowners and customers gaze in amazement. His sales associate brings him a chair and Klaus almost falls as he steps up on top of the chair's seat. "People of Mystic Bay," he shouts. "I want an angel debate with whoever's not chicken! Prove to me that angels really visited this town!!!"

We say goodbye to each other, ignoring him. Bobby comments walking back in the store, "Klaus needs to go back to his law firm. He was actually nicer there if that's possible to believe." Mac shakes his head as they walk upstairs to their offices. Justine stops me before I walk over to *Heaven Can't Wait.* "Ken, I had a dream last night and I think it is prophetic. Miranda is not coming back to town for sure. They've had words. She's over Bobby. I think her ego was damaged, not her love. No, some other man has captured her attention. But Klaus is far from over it. In fact he is riled up now. It's displaced anger. He did this all for her."

"It's hard to believe it's gotten to this point. He's selling a lot of merchandise. I hear people from out of town think it's funny. I can't believe he's still running a law business or is he? His MO screams to me he has to win at all costs and has also spoiled Miranda unmercifully."

"I know, it's sad. It didn't help her life for Klaus to raise her with no work ethic, no gratitude, just a perpetual give me attitude! I'm sure Bobby was so different from the other men she knew. He's laid back, unassuming, giving and unpretentious, and unimpressed with her money. But he did fall for her beauty. She is a stunning woman."

"Beauty is only skin deep as we know, Justine. The inside is the essence of anyone." I say it knowing it to be one of the truest statements ever made.

But Klaus wants to debate about the angel sightings. What is your perception Justine?" I almost know what she will say, but I let her say it to me. She's stronger now; her world is better.

" Well, I'm thinking we should give him what he wants on a silver platter, that's what dear Madam Norma always says. I'll call Madam Norma and Mayor Willie Walin and talk about it. We'll give him his debate somehow and maybe we'll ask July North to be the moderator! It's a great idea isn't it?" Justine has a satisfied look on her face.

"Yes. I like that idea. You all figure it out okay? I'd like to break the news to Klaus. Please tell Madam Norma and Willie. Just tell me when to tell him and all the particulars. He's a bit intimidated by me."

"A big man plus a kind heart? Of course he's intimidated!" We hug goodbye and I walk to my store as little droplets of rain fall, watching Klaus get off his chair still shouting as the crowd disperses. I wonder what suggestions Madam Norma will have in that brilliant head of hers?

A few hours later I walk over to *The Angel and Butterfly Shoppe*. Klaus looks harried and wild eyed as he comes out to meet me. Obviously, he doesn't want me to come in his store and as he looks at me I grow larger and glow. His eyes widen. "Mr. Waxman, I heard you asking for an angel debate, sir, and Mayor Walin has been informed. He is waiting on the Town Council's approval, but sees no problem. If it is approved it will be held in the Mystic Bay High School gym next Saturday evening, six o'clock sharp. July North will be the moderator. Rules will be drawn up by the Town Council and will have to be followed. Does this sound satisfactory?"

To say Klaus Waxman is dumbfounded is not true. He's astounded by the news. "Uh, yes, I guess so. Who's invited?"

His eyes are wilder still and he looks from left to right as if frightened for some reason. The shoppers near the store don't notice.

"Anyone can attend. There will be time limits to speaking however. But after everyone who wants to has spoken then we go around again. It will last approximately two hours." Klaus mutters, "My own attorney will be there for sure and I'm inviting the media. Humph!" Klaus seems to be tongue-tied at that point and so I say a hearty, "Goodbye, Mr. Waxman!" Off I go across the street and back to my store. This will be the best way to solve this issue with all the townsfolk willing to partake in the debate. Justine and the others have big ideas. There will be clips on the news but it's okay. I'm proud of the people here. They trust their instincts.

~~~~~~~~~~~

It's been a whirlwind of a week getting ready for the event. The Town Council approved and July is ready to moderate. A podium is set up complete with a loud speaking system. We heard through the grapevine that Klaus is indeed inviting the news people but Madam Norma in her glory now says, "Bring them on!"

The Mystic Bay High School gym is packed with townsfolk including children. Dan Pica and Tiffany Gould are there. She is the one TV reporter agreed upon. She seems pleased at that. She and I look at each other and she gives me thumbs up. I give it right back. A big network is outside but not invited in the gym, as there isn't enough room to accommodate all their equipment. There's a chill to the air outside but it's nice and warm in the gym. July
~~~~~~~~~~~

North waits at the podium. Near her sits the Mayor and Town Council. Speakers will be able to get up one at a time and speak for two minutes. We angels, including, July, will not give our opinions. This night is for the people of Mystic Bay. There is hope that Klaus Waxman won't be crass or volatile but everyone is being realistic about it.

In the front row sits Madam Norma in her scooter, Jamie Bond, Laurjean, Hannah O'Ryan, Violinist Anthony Chen, his son and others who have chosen to speak. Behind them are Justine and her family and Laurjean's family. Mike and Liz have come home for the debate. The bleachers and the chairs on the floor are full and there is loud talking in anticipation of the event.

Tiffany is interviewing some people on the sidelines, people I don't recognize. Perhaps they are new in town. As the hands on the clock on the wall moves to six, July speaks and quiets the room down. July is a moderator and a seasoned talk show host. She has a presence about her that puts all at ease. Of course her angel voice is soothing and we six other angels send angel wind throughout the gym. Most of us sit in the third row with others in between us as we have done so many times hoping to remain in the shadows unnoticed as before.

"Welcome, everyone to *The Angel Debate*. At a request of one of our business owners, Mr. Klaus Waxman, we are here today to discuss and debate the angel sightings last year with both pro and con viewpoints. Everyone is welcome to speak for two minutes only. Marilyn Thayer will be calling you up by numbers. We welcome Mayor Willie Walin and the Town Council. Thank you for letting us have this debate. We thank Principal Carol for letting us use this wonderful school facility tonight. Please be respectful and turn off your cell phones to airplane mode or off completely. Please do not record this debate or take photos that may disturb others. Also, there will be no cuss words or name-calling permitted. Chief Jim Nero and his police force will escort those who disturb anyone out of the building.

Now let's get started. You received numbers at the door. Those that came first will get to speak first if they so choose. Mr. Tim Thayer is in the audience with a microphone. Those who want to come up and speak can come up here when called or those who want to speak where they are sitting need only to raise their hand. Those in the bleachers will need to come to the podium. Let's begin."

Miss Marilyn says into the microphone, "Number one please!" Violinist, Anthony Chen comes to the podium. "Hello, I'm Anthony Chen and my family and I live in Mystic Bay. I'm a violinist with the San Francisco Symphony. My son, Benny was taught a song to play on the piano last year. Angels came to him in a dream that he feels was totally real. The melody was given to him to play for the world. My son is visually impaired. He has musical gift and is considered a child prodigy. The song he learned is a beautiful melody, which has been heard around the world and has been played at all types of events. It truly is a song from the angels. This is the truth as God is my witness. Angels came to him. Benny has a musical ear and memorized it note for note. Thank you." Klaus is fidgeting in his seat. We all have noticed no one came with him. Miranda is clearly absent showing no support for her overly generous father. If his attorney is here he is unseen. It is quiet in the room with the occasional cough and rustling noise in the seats. Miss Marilyn calls out number two.

Laurjean comes to the podium dressed in an understated beige pantsuit, the pink streaks are gone for the moment, "Hello everyone. I thank you all for the opportunity to speak. I am Laurjean Whitefeather. Most of you know me. My husband and I own *The Next Door Café*. When the children saw angels last year it was truly a miracle. No one has told an untruth. These three children are innocents and told the truth. Before Mr. Chen's son Benny saw and heard an angels song, another boy created angel art beyond his maturity or creativity. These happenings were real. Also, a little girl with disabilities spoke for the first time. It is my belief that the angels chose those with disabilities because they are more open and resonate a pureness. The angel sightings inspired the whole town. Volunteerism is at a record high, adoption and fostering children and animals is widespread in town. There is an angelic mood that has a joy to it. I believe miracles happened in Mystic Bay!" Laurjean leaves saying thank you and returns to her seat.

Number three comes up and it is the Comeback Kid, Jamie Bond. He looks nervous and is dressed in a nice shirt and jeans. I look over and Madam Norma is as pleased as punch with him. Pleased at his demeanor and how he's turned his young life around. She looks at him and gives the thumbs up sign and he begins.

"I'm Jamie Bond of Bondo's Bikes. I just opened my store and I'm really happy about it. This town and the people in it have given me a new life for my family. I believe with all my heart angels really came to Mystic Bay. I know miracles happened. The little kids saw them and that's good enough for me. Kids with disabilities aren't prone to lying. Somehow I know these angels are here with us and have helped me. I can feel it. They sent me my new family, Madam Norma, Miss Marilyn and Tim Thayer. They sent Maggie and her husband, Noah. But mostly they sent me the ability to get my life together and be a better man and a father. Thank you." He sits down and I admire his composure. I admire him for not mentioning that his daughter, Emma Rose, was the child who saw an angel and spoke for the first time. At six she said her first word and it was 'angel.'

There's still rustling and noise but no one is talking. I am so pleased.

Number four stands in the audience. It is Mac. "I'm Mac Jones, new here in Mystic Bay. My granddaughter and I have just moved here and I must say I feel blessed bringing her up in this lovely town. I believe angels came last year because I see our life changing before my very eyes. My granddaughter is happier than she's ever been. I may not have seen angels but I know they are at work here. In all my years living in different places, meeting people from all over the world, I've never encountered such a place with the kindest people on earth. I believe every word about the angels and I know many of you feel the same as I do. Thank you." As he sits down the room begins to hum with conversation. Mac sits down and I'm impressed. He was eloquent and sincere in his statement, but it is not proof. I look over at Tiffany Gould and her small cameraman. They are both really engaged in taking the statements.

Number five is called and it's Klaus Waxman who gets up to the podium. He's sweating, wearing an *I'm No Angel* blue t-shirt. Even a non-psychic or non-angel can tell he's one unhappy man. "I'm Klaus Waxman and owner of *The Angel and Butterfly Shoppe*. I asked for this debate and thus far I've not heard any evidence of any kind that proves angels were here two years ago. Show me an angel, people, show me proof. This town only wanted to make money like that author, Sam Blakley, who got rich off the movie he made from his novel.

People love my *I'm No Angel* t-shirts. They're buying a lot of my gifts. When we talk to people who come in from other areas they all think this is nothing but hogwash and a big sell. Also, Bobby Delany and his family here ruined my daughter Miranda's life. She won't talk to me now and it's entirely their fault. It's not a great town. I've been snubbed by half the people here for sure." There's lots of talking and July breaks in, her voice firm but soothing. "Mr. Waxman please, we asked there be no name calling or harshness of any kind. Please stick to the topic of angels and not make this personal."

Bobby stands, "Excuse me, July, but I have to address Mr. Waxman. I told your daughter I wished her love and happiness and I wish the same for you. The day she asked you for forty thousand dollars in front of me, I knew this was not a relationship for me. She needs help and you have used your store and this platform to try to intimidate my family and me and that's not right. We wish you well but we also wish, for the sake of the town, that you go elsewhere." Bobby, Justine, Pam Ellen, and Bob get up and walk out. Klaus is left standing there as some people start to leave in the bleachers and on the floor. July does not encourage anyone to stay. Klaus stays stationary and angry. Of course he must know that Bobby has been right about his daughter, but who likes to see some things the way they really are? Tiffany probably got this all on camera and I wonder if it will be on the ten o'clock news? We angels sit and don't look at each other noticing Madam Norma has been looking at us on and off. As people file out, Klaus still stays like a bull in a china shop stunned but raring to raise hell.

"Do you have anything else to say, Mr. Waxman?"

"That's not true. My daughter is a good person." He wipes his eyes and leaves the podium saying, "Can I come back up if I want to?"

"Later, yes after everyone else has spoken." July is firm but kind to him.

Number six is called and Madam Norma drives her scooter to the front. Tim brings her the microphone. "Hello, Mr. Klaus Waxman. Do you remember me? Madam Norma Gilbert, the oldest psychic and the oldest lady or gentleman in town, I guess. I get you. I really do. You truly believe this angel thing is all hogwash, but, my dear man, it isn't. It's as true as the sky is blue and true as the rivers run. But to have proof, one sometimes needs to believe. Like love, you can see it in the eyes of people but can you really see tangible love? It's just in the expression of it. So it is with angels. Little Benny saw the angels, so did the little girl and boy with disabilities. Others have seen angels and maybe they will come up and tell us about it. But it's all about believing Mr. Klaus Waxman. I want you to listen to the angel's song. I've asked Principal Carol to play it on the sound system now. I believe you have never heard this song." She is quiet for a moment and the song comes on. I close my eyes listening to the heavenly piano song that has touched the world. People around me pull out tissues and I can hear crying. It is a song of love from above. I open my eyes and look at Klaus. His mad expression has lessoned somewhat and he is staring at Madam Norma. She is staring at him with kind eyes and a purple aura above her bringing peace to my angel being. I look at my fellow angels sitting near me and lovely Angel, July. They are glowing as well, including the soft glow of their halos. I'm glad we left the children with a baby sitter. This has been a tension-filled segment of the debate until the song played.

After the song is over Madam Norma states, "The beauty of the song is as individual as each person. Mr. Waxman. We would like to give you a book sold in our *Angel Museum* in Riverton. It tells the story of the angel sightings with photos of the artwork. The author is my great grandson-in-law, Noah Greenstreet." Tim hands Klaus a book and Klaus takes it but doesn't look at it. "Believe, Mr. Klaus Waxman. It could do you wonders." She leaves the podium area and finds her place again next to Mabel.

Number eight is called and up walks Benny Chen with his father. He has his Service dog with him, his Doberman, Jazzie. Her knowing eyes show only love for Benny. He walks up to the microphone that Tim is holding in front of the crowd. There is a hush as his dog sits down and the boy takes the microphone. "I'm Benny Chen. I am the boy who heard the angel music. My parents don't want me to give interviews so this is not an interview. I saw the angels and I thought it was like a dream but it was real. They were singing. I couldn't really see them, but they glowed. I felt them touch my arms. I have a musical ear and I memorized the song in a few minutes. The angels told me to play the song for the world. That was me playing that you just heard. It is the truth. I will play the song for many people, as I grow older. If the angels come again I will let you know. One more thing…my dog Jazzie was there with me. If only she could talk she'd tell you the same thing. That's all I have to say, Dad." Anthony Chen helps his son and the dog move away. Out the door they go. One fourth of the crowd has left but Klaus obviously isn't leaving. Did Benny make an impact on him? It's hard to tell.

Number seven is called and Doc Lindley stands where he is and Tim walks over to him. "Many of you know me, I'm Dr. Eric Lindley, retired vet. I own the farm on the outskirts of town and my wife and I have rescued deer from a deer farm. One night a month or so ago I was helping a doe give birth. I was having trouble getting the fawn out of his mother. Then the barn lit with an unusual light and I felt hands on my forearms giving me the strength to get the fawn out. All I know is I've seen it before in my practice a few times, someone has been there helping me, invisible, silent and strong. I think it was one or more angels." He sits down and there's a hush in the room. We angels still don't look at each other but I notice Madam Norma glance my way. I look at her and give a half smile.

"Number eight," calls Miss Marilyn and a tall middle-aged black man now stands. I recognize him right away. I sink in the chair as Tim finds him and as he starts to speak a bead of sweat forms on my human angel brow. "I'm Clifford James. I live in Riverton. This happened over fifteen years ago. I was driving down Highway twenty-five from Riverton going south when my truck stopped on that dangerous curve everyone avoids. I got out but since it was a Saturday I had to be careful because cars were whizzing by me. I was afraid and so I stepped to the side. A man immediately pulled up in a tow truck with writing on it that was hard to read. He got out and carefully headed my way. He was a young black man like myself. He was big. Actually, I've always thought he kinda looked a little like Ken Leighton over there. Sorry, Coach, but you do look a lot like him." I nod and smile, terrified. "He wore overalls but with a name tag on him that I couldn't read, either. He told me he would look at my car and asked me to stand in front, so cars would see me and not hit us. I couldn't see what he was doing. In less than a few minutes he fixed my car. I couldn't believe it; he had no tools with him. I told him thanks and he quickly said goodbye, got into his tow truck and left. As he drove away and I started to get into my truck, I noticed all the cars were driving slower, like slow motion. I found I could get back out on to the road easier. When I did get on the road the cars went fast again as before.

That's my story and I've always felt like he was my angel. Where'd the guy come from? How did he fix my car so fast? Wouldn't let me pay him either. It just seemed more than a coincidence." I don't dare look at the other angels. Clifford Jones goes back to his seat. He waves to me and says, "Sorry Coach, I didn't know you lived near me. Love the Shakers; we sure miss you as the coach now. Not doing well this year!" Everyone laughs and some applaud and I shrink a little more. I didn't think my past angel help would catch up with me. I didn't know I'd be living my human experience. I smile and wave back. A few people turn to look at me and I smile.

But July is quick, "Wow, what a great story. Who else has had a story like that where you might have encountered an angel as a human?" The irony of it all makes me nervous but the room rustles with talking and as number ten is called I relax again. I had forgotten my past might be brought forth by some people I've helped a long the way. No one recognized me ever as an angel when I worked for the San Francisco Shakers. Tim holds the microphone for the next person. Fortunately, I don't recognize her.

"I'm Marianna Guttering, I live in Riverton too. One day my husband and I are standing with our three year old daughter, Katie, in our back yard. She points up in the sky and says, 'I see an angel.' We didn't see the angel ourselves but our little daughter held her arms to the heavens and said, 'Glory Hallelujah!' She'd never said those words before. She's twenty now and it's still unbelievable to all of us. She swears she saw an angel wearing a white robe with shiny wings."

Marianna takes her seat and everyone begins talking again. It's getting close to the time to leave. I find myself hoping no one else comes forward so I can run home and not be fearful someone is going to recognize one of us. We've all had lives helping people as angels. July and January have dyed their hair and don't look the same. Taylor and I are older and Donnie and Josh came as angel children to their families all those years ago. Taylor and I helped many as a tag team.

Next, an old man rises. " I'm Paul Whitman. I work over at Phil's Christmas Trees. Years ago I was in the Navy. I was swimming off Coronado Island. There was an undertow and I started to drown. My buddy was on the beach and didn't see me but as I went under I felt an arm grab me and someone pulled me to shore. When I reached shore no one was there in the water with me. My friend ran up to me. He told me it was like someone had tied a rope to my arm and pulled me to shore. He said he was so frozen in shock he couldn't move. To this day we talk about it. Was it an angel who saved my life? We couldn't see who but someone or angel was pulling me!" He sits down and everyone begins talking again. Klaus rises and asks July, "May I say something?"

July says, "As long as no one else has anything to say yes." No once else raises their hand and after a minute she tells Klaus to go ahead.

"I am an attorney and an attorney's duty is to find facts. You have given me no facts today. I feel you all have ignored my store. I'm not budging. I have a good following of tourists and sell many of my products on line. People overseas love my t-shirts. I feel you are a delusional town. As for you, Mr. Chen, your son had a dream. Since he is obviously gifted, his mind produced a beautiful song that is all."

Klaus gets up to leave but Madam Norma puts an arm up to stop him. She beckons him over. I hear with my angel ear what she whispers to him. "Please don't go, Mr. Waxman. I understand your feelings and as July stated you are entitled to your beliefs of course." Amazingly, Klaus goes back to his seat. July asks, "Does anyone have a question for Mr. Waxman?" The crowd is quiet as no one wants to speak. We angels won't interfere. "Then shall we end our debate even though it's under our two hour limit? I want to thank each of you for coming and participating. This has been interesting and as uplifting for me as I hope it has for all of you."

There is applause and people start to leave. Since I'm near the front I see Mike get up. " If I can July, I would like a word with Mr. Waxman." July asks Klaus if it would be all right and he agrees. Tim takes the microphone to Mike. " Hello Mr. Waxman, I am Mike Greer, a resident here and a student at UCLA. I would like a private word with you, Ken Leighton and Madam Norma tonight. It will only take a few minutes to ask you a question. Would that be agreeable to you?"

Klaus Waxman is caught off guard. No one else has spoken to him personally except Madam Norma. People are leaving in quiet conversation as they go out of the building. Madam Norma is still nearby. Miss Marilyn, Tim and Jamie move back waiting by the door for Madam Norma. Tiffany is waiting by the door also interviewing people. She probably is waiting for Klaus and Madam Norma. The microphones are turned off and volunteers are taking down the equipment. People have moved away now with soft chatter. Klaus looks nervous under the lights, he's still sweating but looks around at the crowd leaving. I have a feeling what Mike will say. We approach Klaus Waxman and Mike and I sit in the chairs along side Madam Norma and Klaus. The kind and psychic young man begins, " Mr. Waxman, I wanted to speak with you, Madam Norma and Ken alone. You see they know that I am a psychic. My ability is the only one I know of here in Mystic Bay. Upon occasion I see animal spirits that have passed away to the heaven realm, yet remain near their people. You had a big black dog named Freddy you loved and when you were in law school he passed away. You weren't home at the time and it has saddened you all your life. You wished somehow you could have taken him to the vet but you couldn't. You didn't know he was sick. You have always felt responsible. It changed your life in many ways but I want you to know Freddy is with you always. He, like your guardian angel, walks with you sending love each day." Instantly, I see Klaus' guardian angel. He transmits to me his name is Kindheart. He is eight feet tall and sad, for his eyes are closed. Then he is gone in a whip of light. Klaus stands, "This is really low and outrageous for you to bring up my dog. You have seen photos of me somewhere or talked to Miranda or someone I know!"

"No Mr. Waxman this is the real deal and there's more. The dog also is with a cat, an orange cat named Tyrone. They are inseparable. They speak by sending feelings to you now, they send you only love and good wishes."

Klaus has tears in his eyes. He sits down hard in his seat. "Someone told you this! Who was it?"

Mike is gentle but firm. "I am sorry to hurt you, I don't mean to. This is evidence Mr. Waxman, evidence of the life beyond. I have one more thing to say to you. Then if you don't believe me, I have tried my best. You had a quiet name for your animals that no one ever heard but you, Freddy and Tyrone. You called them 'my pals' for you had a sad childhood Mr. Waxman. They were your unconditional love. That's why you never could get another animal. You were heart broken when they left the earth but they really never left you at all, Sir." Mike stands, kisses Madam Norma on the cheek saying goodbye. He walks out without another word. Madam Norma and I are left quietly looking at Klaus. Klaus is motionless staring into space. Madam Norma places her hand on his. He weeps; his hands go to his face.

I get up to leave and say, "You have good in your soul, Klaus. There are angels and spirits of those we love all around us. I'm sure of it. If you ever need to talk, I'm here."

I join the others outside and we silently head back to our homes. Tiffany Gould wants an interview with us but I hold up my hand and shake my head no. I am proud of Mike. He was eloquent, kind and determined to share what he knows. It had an impact. I am even more than proud of my flock, the townsfolk of Mystic

Bay. They let Klaus speak his mind. That is the epitome of freedom.

Chapter 12

Klaus and Madam Norma

Our flying at night was wondrous! Main Street was wet, as a slight rain had fallen as if to sweep all negative thoughts and heaviness away. Everyone was pleased with the debate and how people were respectful to Klaus. He had no one with him. Not even the daughter he tried to defend would stand by his side. We see him speed away in his Mercedes toward his lonely condo on Westminster Hill. We send him wishes for a safe journey home. I feel he needs me somehow, as he's such a sad human. He needs love energy sent to him as his guardian angel has transmitted to him to no avail. Sturdy walls of anger and despair have been built in his mind.

The air is chilly but not to angels like us. It's just Gabe, Donnie and me tonight floating and flying up and down in pure delight. Our mission for the town is done for now. We know it's only a matter of time until Klaus closes his shop, as Justine and Pam Ellen predict. Over the soft lights of the boats in the heart shaped harbor of Mystic Bay I soar with my friends, never wanting our flight to end. The sea sprays mist in our faces, the stars shine and the silent falling stars remind us of the magnificence of the heavens. It's time to say goodnight. We fly over the roofs of town to our perspective homes. Klaus' Guardian Angel Kindheart transmitted mentally to me that Klaus must be left to his own free will now. Of course, I agree I can only whisper guidance or show him the way using nature or sending love and kindness on angel wind. Perhaps he will find peace on his own with a word or two from someone with good intentions.

83

Tonight, Val is staying at Mac's and I miss him, but Barty is here to greet me as I turn in. My bed is soft and warm and the curtains flutter in the cool breeze of the sea coming in the open window. The chill of the night air soothes me as I take in angel human breath saying, thank you to Him who sent me here. He created the love and the beauty on the planet and all the dear humans who fight for justice and love. Reflecting back on the event of this evening, I think of my conversation with Mike afterward. I told him how proud his father is of him as he truly believes in the heaven realm and I am sure Ned was watching with love, his spirit surrounding Mike. "I felt him near me tonight," Mike told me. "He never understood psychic ways but now he knows the mind is part of the mystery of life. Having you there with me and having Madam Norma there helped me tonight. I saw the pain in Klaus Waxman's eyes but I knew I must tell him about his animal companions for he has suffered terribly these many years since childhood. This is why he spoiled Miranda, I guess. He never wanted her to go without like he did. He wanted her to feel his love but it backfired. He smothered her with material things and no rules or values were given. He wouldn't let her have an animal companion. I saw it all. Sometimes it comes to me like rain falling so fast I have to ask the angels to slow it down!"

Mike and I said goodnight and he walked to his house with Justine and Liz arm and arm. That's what family is all about. I'm overwhelmed with love; I have a human family of my own now. "Val," I whisper. "Goodnight!" I fall asleep fast and when I awake I know the heaviness of negativity has left the town. I know in my angel heart as Val rushes in the door to greet me, that love has found it's way in to help sorrow as it always does.

It's Sunday and my turn to work at the store. The kids will be with Justine most of the day having lunch and painting. *The Angel and Butterfly Shoppe* has a closed sign up. I sell my angel wares all day and everyone remarks how beautiful the luminous angel paintings of Justine's are with butterflies on their shoulders. Customers are commissioning Justine to paint faces of their loved ones on the angels. How dear it is really!

Mike and Liz are having lunch at *The Next Door Café* with Justine, Mac, Billie Jo and Val. The twins stop in to say goodbye before they drive back to L A. in their new car. It's hard for Justine to see them go but she is painting again and has found a new purpose helping Mac and me with the children. I get a call from Madam Norma to stop over for tea and sandwiches when I close shop at five, so I ask Justine to keep Val a while longer for me.

Deciding to walk the short distance to her house at 20 Moon Road, I admire the hanging baskets on the lampposts on Main Street. They are filled with geraniums and sweet alyssum, some hang on the storefronts too. The stucco and brick walls of the stores beckon all in everyday with their welcoming signs and kind souls.

Donnie is at the door of *The Next Door Café* wiping his hands on his apron. He's finished his work for the day. "My friend," he says politely to me. He knew with angelic sense, I was coming by his restaurant as he cleaned up finishing the homemade bread he made for tomorrow morning. He or Laurjean always stand outside before and after they open or close the café for the day. They are tired from their hard work but love to look at the faces walking down Main Street and the goings on around the stores as the sun starts sinking down amidst the wisps of clouds. I'm in anticipation of what Madam Norma will have to say.

On the other side of Main street Taylor and Gabe are standing outside Gabe's store, *Dear Dogs Etc.* "Hello Ken," Gabe calls. His pet squirrel, the comical Bubbles, is on his shoulder chattering to those who walk by. Taylor waves. It strikes me funny that no one walking down Main Street has a clue they've just encountered four angels living as humans in our fair little town by the sea.

Bobby is walking down the street too. He stops, "Hey Ken, I'm on my way back from Madam Norma's. We had a super talk about last night. She's one wise lady, I tell you."

"That she is, Bobby,"

"I'm going to get a rescue dog when I move into my new house. I signed a contract today for a neat ranch on Meadowbrook Lane. It's a big yard. Maybe I'll get two dogs or three." He laughs and it's good to see him full of happiness.

"Good idea. I think all who love animals should have at least one dog or cat or more. I may get another for Val and Barty. They soothe our souls and we are the keepers of their souls."

"Ken, you always have a way of talking that blows my mind; so spiritual, really. No wonder you helped all those football players. I hear many of them are helping you with your volunteer program. I'd like to help, too. I see how Justine's involvement with Val and Billie Jo has impacted her in such a positive way."

"Yes, Bobby. We'd love your help. It's those angel miracles!" I smile to myself as we say goodbye and he walks on. Knowing I was near, July and January walk out of Mystic Bay Bakery coming toward me pushing Heather in a stroller. Spencer is happily walking beside them with a bag full of goodies. They've been invited to Gabe's house for dinner and they're taking the kids to see Bubbles perform her nutty antics. That squirrel could have his own TV show. They wave to me. I turn down Moon Road toward the sea; the sea birds fly by in poetic syncopation and the trees sway away from fall sea breezes. Madam Norma's house is white with blue shutters. The white sign with gold lettering out front says *Madam Norma's Parlor.* As I walk up the stairs, Doc Josh comes out the door. The handsome angel must have known I was coming. "Hi Ken, go on in the house. Madam Norma's inside, she's expecting you. I was just giving King a shot because Madam Norma can't come over to the office. King is under the weather." He whispers. "I sent him a little angel dust to relax him this afternoon." He resumes speaking normally, " Miss Marilyn and Tim left for a few days vacation. Her housekeeper, Mabel, is staying with her and making tea for Madam Norma and you." Josh whispers, "See you Saturday night, Ken." He winks, walks down the stairs, and the door opens.

Mabel, the housekeeper, welcomes me in. "Madam Norma is in the backyard sitting in her favorite glider. Right this way, please." Telling her thank you, Mabel leads me through to the kitchen and out the back door. I notice the old dog named Cookie, sleeping dreamily in her bed near the stove. I walk out into the most beautiful garden in Mystic Bay. The yard is filled with fragrant flowers. Entomologists have been here in her yard and the surrounding yards and also in July's yard on the cliff. They are researching the newest species of bee found in the area. The bees are elusive.

Mabel says, "I have banana bread and tea sandwiches Maggie made. Would you like some?"

"Sounds wonderful, thank you!" Mabel goes back in the kitchen and I find Madam Norma sitting in her glider with eyes closed, napping. A flashback makes me pause remembering Maggie, her great granddaughter, and her husband, Noah, watched we angels fly the night of the eclipse. Good thing they remember us now as only a lovely dream. I walk over.

"Well dear Ken, I'm so glad you're here." Madam Norma wears blue pants, blouse and shoes matching the rest of the Robin's egg blue sky. King, her dog, is at her side on a dog bed. He is a little lethargic, obviously napping, as usually he is up at once to greet guests. He opens one eye and shuts it again in lingering slumber. "Take a seat, dear Ken."

"You did a wonderful job last night. You were comforting and kind and straight forward, Madam Norma. I admire you." Madam Norma looks away toward the sea. The big Bishop Pine sways and I smell it's powerful pine scent and feel its majestic beauty.

"And your presence was a comfort to me. You know, Ken I am tired these last few weeks. This all has been trying. I have a favor to ask of you."

"Of course, Madam Norma. Anything you ask, I will do, you

know that."

Mabel brings out the tea, sandwiches and banana bread. "Thank you," Madam Norma tells her sweetly. She pours us each a cup. I take mine with a bit of milk like Madam Norma does. We each take our first sip and put our teacups back on the saucers.

"Klaus Waxman is coming over in a little while. He knows you will be here. I would like you to mentor him as you did all those football players. I want you to take him under your wing." She looks at me and I hope my shock doesn't show on my face.

"Well of course, yes, if you want but Madam Norma he doesn't seem to care much for me. Maybe someone else would be better, someone ah…" I'm finding I can't finish the sentence. Why? Does she know? I get ahold of myself. "Does he want my help?"

Madam Norma looks at me with those knowing eyes of hers. "If you could just see what I see. I will be there with you most of the time, but I see a frightened man who was a frightened boy with no love to speak of. He created a hardened shell. He met his wife and thought his world had bloomed like a flower in the spring. Then she was gone and he had a child to raise besides building a budding law practice. He made many mistakes with Miranda and he's tangled up his own life something grand." Tears form in her eyes. "I will be with you, but well, I have a reason I'm asking you." She doesn't elaborate. She knows I'm an angel. I'm sure of it now.

"I will do my best. You know I will."

Madam Norma looks at me with the slight, beautiful smile of the wisest woman I have ever known. The love for her family was evident as she raised her daughter, granddaughter and great granddaughter, too. She's counseled lots of people in town helping to change many a life, including Jamie Bond's. I have to ask her the boldest question. "Did you ask the angels to help Klaus also for we all have a guardian angel?" I'm testing her and I can't help it. I'm suspicious more than ever. A flock of sea birds fly swishing over the yard as the sun starts to set. We stop and stare as the sky brightens to an orange sherbet color, and it awes us both with its beauty.

"Yes," she finally says. "I've asked his guardian angel and all the other angels to help and I know they will now." She looks directly in my eyes with that knowing look of hers and I almost gulp my tea down and stuff the slice of banana bread in whole! She'll require an angel dusting if she knows.

The back door opens and Klaus walks behind Mabel. He looks shaken and somewhat irritated. "Hello, Madam Norma," Klaus says quietly.

"Oh Klaus, please take a seat dear. You know Ken Leighton, I'm sure?" I extend my hand and Klaus surprisingly takes mine. "Yes," is all he says, yet he averts his eyes. Mabel leaves, but as Klaus sits down she briskly brings another cup of tea and more banana bread. He settles in, looking around the yard.

"Klaus, you know I asked Ken here because I think you need another friend in this town besides me. Ken has been here over ten years and knows everyone. I would like him to do some sharing of his knowledge with you. He's done life coaching with football players and helps many children in his Bay Area Sports Program. Would you agree to schedule three afternoon chats with Ken and me of course?"

"Madam Norma, I don't know," He finally looks at me and seems surprised. Maybe he's surprised I didn't seem to grow larger or glow. " I don't know."

Madam Norma doesn't say anything.

I say, "I am willing to meet, Mr. Waxman, if you agree. Madam Norma is the wisest woman I have ever met and she has a feeling you would benefit from talking to us both. I've worked with many adults and children and I sense you have family issues. Of course, I could leave right now and would never tell a soul. That's who I am."

" I asked Ken here to be with us, Klaus, because when you apologized for being rude to me I realized time is of the essence. I feel you need help in your relationship with Miranda. And you heard the angel stories last night. I know you told me you still don't believe they're real, but Ken here knows more about angels then anyone in town. He owns *Heaven Can't Wait*, the angels' store. He's never told me but I get the feeling he really does see angels."

As Klaus looks at me with questioning eyes, I'm taken aback. I say nothing, as she really didn't ask me. She just made a statement.

I don't know." That's all Klaus says looking at her, not me.

"We can meet right here at my home on Tuesdays when my daughter, Marilyn and her husband Tim are at work either morning or afternoon every week. Why, it's just me here with Mabel then. King here is a sweet boy and old Cookie; our other dog sleeps all day in the kitchen. I'll be in on most of your meetings if you'd like but I think it'd be good to talk man to man without me at some point. Ken is more in touch with the angels and has many an angel story to tell, I'm sure."

She looks at me again and I keep my angel composure in check. She and I have never discussed angels except the sighting last year. "Madam Norma, you always know the angels are around," I say.

"Yes, dear Ken, but you have a distinct gift. You have an angel store. You tell us the angel stories customers have told you. You seem never to doubt angels exist for one moment and I have a psychic feeling you see them." She looks at me with the wise eyes of an owl, wide and piercing yet in kindly beauty. No one has ever suggested to me I have seen angels in my ten years here.

Looking at Klaus with slight trepidation," Well, I might have encountered angels; I know a few incidents where it may have occurred. But Mr. Waxman, I must ask you, do you wonder, even a small bit, if angels might exist after our debate?"

Klaus looks down on the ground. "Not yet," he says, then

looking up, "I'll think about it but nothing more. I'm closing the shop and that will take a lot of work." There is only silence for a moment.

"I'll let you know," Klaus says with a shrug.

"Tuesdays would be the best time," says Madam Norma and I think to myself how dear it could be, Tuesdays with the angel. Looking up I see Kindheart translucent and filled with love for his human. His magnificent form disappears in a whip of light and I look back before anyone notices I've been staring at him.

"Let us know when you can," Madam Norma smiles. "I'll make sure we have lots of banana or pumpkin bread for you both. We can sit in the garden if it's warm and sunny enough or my parlor for privacy." She takes Klaus's hand. "This will be a good step for you, Klaus, a really good step."

Do I see a bit of fear in Klaus' eyes? He is suspicious of me, I'm sure. "Here is my card, Sir." I will determine what to say or what not to say to him. It may be no different than how I converse with anyone old or young who needs my guidance.

Madam Norma says, "Please, think of questions you want to ask us. Write them down if you want and bring a recorder and record anything you want. You are my main focus now, young man." She smiles and I am more in awe of this special psychic human then anyone I have ever known. Her brilliance shines, but not as much as her kindly ways. "By the way was your mother's name Ruth?" Madam Norma is confident she is correct.

Klaus' look is one of surprise, but then his face softens. "Yes, it would be in the records of my birth."

"Yes," replies, the treasured Madam Norma. "Somehow, I feel her presence." Klaus looks anguished. "I have to leave now."

"Of course."

Waving to Klaus as he takes off in his black Mercedes, I walk back to my home perplexed. Why isn't Madam Norma handling

Klaus herself? She has a relationship with him in a motherly way. She sees his mother's spirit while I'm just a big ex- football coach to him. I've used my glowing and growing larger to awe Klaus really almost scaring him? I won't even tell the other angels about this. This is something I must do on my own if he ever does want to meet. She must have her plan and I'm finding she knows the secret I'm an angel and is using it to help Klaus. Viewing the beauty of dusk now walking down Main Street, I see angels near their humans, walking beside them or floating above. Oh, if Klaus could see the majesty of this sight or know his angel is always near sending him light. He needs to talk to us and reflect to let go. Everyone needs someone like Madam Norma, and everyone needs to know the angels are near. As the sun sets and night begins to fall, the walking is good for me. I could choose to be home. Instead, I love being around the tourists and townsfolk as they stroll, as if in a parade going to dinner, or talking to the storeowners as they close their shops.

Stopping to look around, no one is looking at me, so I disappear from sight and instantly I'm in Klaus' car next to him. Of course he's unaware. Looking at him I send peaceful angel wind and love to him. I see him sigh and look my way for a moment. Does he sense me? No, but he must wonder why an intense feeling of peace has come. Instantly, I'm walking back on Main Street again. No one saw me materialize, of course. As light dims and I get home, Mac steps out of his door and asks me to come over for dinner. He and Justine have made spaghetti for us. Hugging my son while smelling the fine dinner they've prepared, I find myself jovial and uplifted knowing I've more work to do, not only with children but, hopefully I'll help Klaus somehow, too. We laugh as we eat dinner together, a happy outcome to a different kind of day. We play with the dogs as they run through the kitchen and I ponder how I didn't see this day coming. Angels can't predict, only soften and guide lives if humans will let them. If Klaus is willing to meet, will I know what to say? Yes, I think, if I can help the bullying ways of many a young testosterone filled male, I can help a man with so many issues stemming from a lost childhood. God, the angels and knowledge of the vast stars and planets of the universe will guide me. All I really know is how to give kindness.

Chapter 13

Tuesday With an Angel

Klaus has packed up his store and today the sign is being taken down. It's been a week and no word from him. Since the day is cloudy and chilly, Madam Norma and I sit on in her parlor. Tea has been laid out with banana bread and pumpkin muffins. She and I decided to meet every Tuesday hoping Klaus will call us to set up an appointment. "We can put our thoughts for him out there to God and the Universe. He needs us, dear Ken."

"Yes, I know. Shall I go to San Francisco to his office? I'm contemplating today would be a good day."

"Good idea. Tell me one of your angel sightings. I know you've seen angels, dear. I feel it."

My angel composure has returned so I say with no trepidation this time. "I've seen them flying, Madam Norma. I've seen them materialize. They are so beautiful, each one different from the next. Their wings are a variety of sliver, gold and all the colors of the rainbow. They shine at night; they glow with halos around their heads. That is all I can tell you." I'm telling the truth and it feels good to me, as I'm not really telling her I'm an angel only that I have seen them. Of course I will sprinkle angel dust when she's not looking later so she forgets the details of my conversation. I don't tell her that her angel is right behind her, a beautiful angel that is so luminous it is hard to make out her features. Her wings are the colors of the sky yet shimmer in the light from the window. She has a glow that is mesmerizing. Her arms are around Madam Norma but there is a tear, I think I see running down her

95

cheek. "You looked worried there for a moment, Ken. You were staring out in space."

"Yes, worried and woeful, too. I'll go to San Francisco today and try to talk to Klaus if I can find him." Madam Norma's angel is gone in a whip of light and we finish our conversation and tea with talk of our families. "You are my treasure, Ken. Thank you for your honesty today. I knew you saw angels and I needed to hear it. You are the only friend I know who has."

"I never tell an untruth, Madam Norma." I smile and hug her as the angel dust comes from my hands. I wave them a bit. "I wish you had described them to me," she sighs honestly. Some day, dear Norma, I think to myself.

Mabel walks in to refresh our tea, but I tell her how wonderful the bread and tea was and that I must leave. I kiss Madam Norma on the cheek. King walks me to the door as he's regained his spunk once again. The sun is trying it's hardest to peek out of the clouds as I get in to my car. Val is in school so I park my car at the beach and get out, admiring the waves and the beauty of God's Earth. I look around and I'm the only one on the beach within eyesight. I close my eyes and instantly I find myself where Klaus is located at *DiMaggio's Place* in downtown San Francisco. A piano player is playing a melody of oldies. Klaus is sitting alone at the bar drinking beer. Alcohol is his nemesis, I'm guessing. I walk up and sit down. He's startled to see me. "How did you know I was here?" He grumbles although I see some sign of relief in his eyes

"I heard you come here some mornings. Am I correct?"

"Sometimes."

"Well, Madam Norma and I are meeting on Tuesday mornings and we did this morning. We hope you will meet with us next Tuesday. It's very pleasant to meet for an hour and have tea or coffee, fruit bread and talk."

Klaus looks at me with weariness. I decide to glow a little and send angel wind and light filled with joy.

"I don't have anything to say." He gulps his beer down. The bartender pours him another and asks me what I want. "Lemonade, thanks."

"Okay, say you don't have anything to say, but I do. Shall I go or can I tell you just a few things I know?"

I glance up at Klaus' angel and he nods. Klaus doesn't say a word and I begin. "I've worked with football players for years and my focus now is on children in group homes or living in shelters. I feel emphatically angels are near us, guiding us somehow all the time. I believe we all have a guardian angel near. Yours is here with you. I'm sure of it. They send love to us. When you are alone you can talk to him and he will help you find your answers. I know this for sure. I'm not a psychic or sensitive. I'll stop now, and if you want to talk come next Tuesday to see us. We'll be waiting." I drink my lemonade and put a twenty on the bar. Klaus doesn't look up.

"Goodbye and take care." I walk outside to the business district where busy people in corporate attire walk quickly as the sky above turns brighter. I'm wondering if Klaus will ever come to see us. He is a lonely man tumbling down a hill. I don't know if I've made any impact. I walk to a side street where no one is looking and disappear instantly back at the beach finding my mind clear but my heart sad. Taking in a big angel human breath, my hope is renewed seeing fish jumping and noticing people are clustering down at the further end of the beach toward the harbor. A blustery wind has picked up. Til next Tuesday, I say to Klaus in my mind. In prayer I whisper, "Help him be there."

98

Chapter 14

Time is A River

They called me to 20 Moon Road. I hadn't seen her smiling face in a week. Doc Nathan is at Madam Norma's bedside. The old dog, Cookie, is on her bed with eyes closed and forlorn King, with his animal instinct, is curled in his bed at her bedside. Miss Marilyn, Maggie, Noah and Tim are with her their faces showing such heartbreak. They're saying goodbye for Madam Norma is leaving the Earth Realm. She's over one hundred now and will miss her next birthday by just a few days. I am overwhelmed with angel and human sadness and tears roll down my cheeks for the first time since I heard Val's sad story of abuse. I have been so drawn to this indomitable spirit, this woman who has taught me more about human beings than anyone else. I love her positive faith and ability to see potential in anyone.

"Mother wants to talk to you alone and we will be right outside the door." Miss Marilyn is brave; her bond with her mother has been solid for seventy plus years. Maggie is weeping and her husband holds her tight as they leave the room.

I sit on the bed next to the fragile, kind woman. "Ken," she says in a weakened voice. I lean down to hear her. "My beautiful angel is waiting for me. And you are so beautiful. I figured it out, the truth, dear angel. Your secret is safe." There's a twinkle for a moment in her blue eyes. My tears fall. I close my eyes in prayer.

"I have one request of you."

"Anything," I tell her taking her delicate hand.

"Meet with Klaus. Don't give up. Tell him I'll be near."

"Yes, dear sweet Madam Norma, I will."

"I'll be seeing you," she says as she closes her eyes. I whisper to her and send angel wind of love surrounding her to comfort her in her final moments left.

" Madam Norma, you have been a good soul for the Earth like the falling rain and golden sun. You are an angel on Earth. I love you." My heart is heavy knowing the everyday of our relationship has changed forever. Her family is weeping as they walk back in. I kiss her on the forehead. As I leave the room so their final time is private, I hear Miss Marilyn say, "It's okay, Mother to go to Dad and the angels." Then I hear her say, "Cookie is going. She will go to be with Mother." Twilight has come and the house is dark except for one light in the parlor. Madam Norma's guardian angel stood near and will guide her home. I wait on the couch. Mabel has come out of kitchen with tea for me. Her eyes show she has been crying. She sets down the tea now and I motion for her to sit by me. She does and I put my arm around her shoulder. "I said my goodbye to her before you came. I didn't want to be there when she passes. Did you know she took me and my kids in from a shelter, gave me a job, found an apartment for my kids and me. She's been my angel."

"I know, Mabel. She was an angel to all of us. But now her spirit will be with you always. That will never change. May you find comfort in that. Miss Marilyn and Maggie still need you. You are part of the family now." Mabel looks appreciative. She wipes her eyes and we sit. My eyes close for a few moments. I take a sip of tea. It takes me back remembering my ten years of friendship with Madam Norma. Now, I finally realize how much of an impact she had on the town with her wiley ways and her incredible mind, a gift to us all. She has been my teacher, too.

I wait awhile until the family comes out of the room. Doc

Nathan and I shake hands. "A great woman is gone." His tears say it all. I embrace the family. I learned that at the exact moment of Madam Norma's passing her lovely dog, Old Cookie, left this world too. Of course, animals go to heaven and so Madam Norma and Cookie will be together in the great beyond.

Chapter 15

The Song of Heaven

Walking home alone, I wonder how humans get along with a piece of their love light gone? I hope I know now. They have their memories and nothing can ever take away memories of love. I stop in at Justine's. She and Mac are making dinner for us again. Val and Billie Jo play with the dogs outside. They rush in to greet me and we tell them the sad news. "Why do people die?" Val asks.

"To be with God and the angels, son. That's where we all will go."

Mac adds, "Everyone will be together. All of us go at separate times."

"Like Grandma?" Billie Jo is worried. She loved her grandmother so and she died while they were trying to gain custody. "Yes, Sweetie, she'll be waiting for us. But we have a lot of living to do." We hug the children and dogs and Mac says wisely, "Believe everything will be good in heaven. Remember those little children saw angels here and it was a miracle. The little boy played a song the angels gave him while he dreamed."

Val looks up with wide eyes, "That's right, but will we see Madam Norma again, Dad?"

"Yes, my dear son. We will all be together. Believe in angels as I do." We talk on for a while saying a prayer for Madam Norma and her dog, Cookie. We spend the rest of the evening together playing children's games. Then Mac and I decide it's time to take the kids home. Justine hugs the children Mac and me as we leave.

The night is cool and the moon is full. Somewhere Madam Norma is pleased about that. She also predicted what I'm seeing now. Justine and Mac have formed a bond since taking care of the children together and it's good to see her happy. She's found she's needed more than she ever thought, a motherly figure to two children who have lived without that special love only a mother or grandmother can give. I see happiness in Val and Billie Jo's faces. Their faces light up when they see her. They paint with her each week now and display their work in the windows of our shops. How lovely it is to watch. It's never too late to learn and grow, we angels always say. But also, it's never too late to find love.

Chapter 16

Life Like Love Is Never Ending

We are on the beach near Madam Norma's Parlor. As family, friends and townsfolk who knew of her gather, Reverend Manual begins, "Today we say goodbye to the woman who was the first born in our lovely town of Mystic Bay one hundred and one years ago today. She was born at home and her father organized the first school in town. She raised a family here with her good husband, Joe Gilbert. Her whole life was devoted to doing good deeds with love. She told me over and over again, love to her was all that matters. Today as her wonderful family, her daughter, Miss Marilyn, Maggie, her great granddaughter and their husbands, Tim and Noah, and Jamie Bond, who she loved as a son, and King, her faithful dog, mourn her loss, they are abundantly aware that her life has only ended here on this earth. She is with God in the mystery of heaven that we all will find someday. Her other faithful old dog, Cookie, passed away, lying with her on her bed the moment she went to our Maker. We know her spirit soars with her husband and dog. So do not mourn long for her, for she told me before she died she'd been waiting a long time for this moment. She loved and admired all of you in Mystic Bay and wishes you all the love and good things life can bring. Let a good life in. You all deserve it. "

Jamie Bond walks up and stands by Reverend Manuel with notes in hand. He takes the microphone. "I loved Madam Norma. She will always be the mother I never had, my friend, and my confidant. She believed in me. She was my life's teacher, encouraging me to be kind and use my potential. Along with Miss

105

Marilyn, whom I love like a second mother, I was given a gift of being taught manners, decency, obligation and thankfulness. I changed my ways, became a good father to Emma Rose and a good co-parent to Elena. I will miss Madam Norma Jean Gilbert all the days of my life. Thank you, Madam Norma, for all you did for me so my life could change to a good one!"

The wind picks up a bit as Jamie moves back to the crowd and Madam Norma's great granddaughter, Maggie, comes up. The dark haired beauty is psychic herself. She hears the hum of life in nature and communicates with all living things especially trees. "My GG was my inspiration. She and Gram raised me. Grand Dad was with us for a while, but died when I was three. His spirit came to me once. One day as GG and I sat in the garden last year, her eyes closed. I feared she had passed away but she was just asleep. When I relayed my fears to her, she told me that one day when it was my time to go to heaven, she would meet me in the center of a rose. So everyday I will remember her as I gaze at the garden's roses that bloom continually. She will be remembered not only as a gifted psychic but for her quiet strength, the nicest and most loving person who ever graced our town."

As Anthony Chen comes forward to play his violin, Justine whispers to me, "Madam Norma's granddaughter is one of those standing by the parking lot, listening. Klaus Waxman will be coming shortly, too, and will stand near her." Justine doesn't look back, yet her abilities give her this knowledge. I ponder how Polly Ann, who now calls herself, Lyla Jasmine, and Klaus don't know each other and never will, but are saying their last goodbyes to a great woman who impacted both their lives. Do they both have regrets?

I turn back to see the small crowd gathered in the parking lot. A beautiful blonde woman stands out. I recognize her from the photo at Madam Norma's. I see Klaus' Mercedes drive up and I turn back to listen to some of the most beautiful music ever played. Anthony Chen is playing the song the angels sang to his son, Benny, in a dream, *Forever Peace, Forever Love*. The clouds seem to drift away with the music. As if on cue, dolphins, leap in the waves. A flock of birds fly by and the people on the beach hold hands. Justine, Pam Ellen, Bob, Bobby and I hold hands with Mike, Liz and Mac. As the music ends, I see Klaus has moved as Justine predicted, right next to Polly Ann. I know I should go and so I walk up past the others toward Klaus. He sees me then and waves one wave. Polly Ann turns to look at me and I nod as she moves back to her car. The woman estranged from her family brought so much hurt to her grandmother, Madam Norma, her mother, Miss Marilyn and her own daughter, Maggie. She came to say goodbye but didn't have enough courage to see her family. She stood back in the background so regretful feelings could only touch her briefly. Then a hopeful sign, her guardian angel, Francis, flies to her car to be with her.

"Hello, Klaus, It's good to see you again." I don't put my hand out for fear he won't take it. "It's good of you to come. It's a beautiful day to honor a kind soul like Madam Norma."

"I got your message. I should've come to see her last Tuesday like she wanted. I…" He stops talking and I wait a moment to tell him, " She told me to tell you she will always be near. You can talk to her still. She'll be listening. She asked me to meet with you if you would be willing."

"I don't believe in heaven." There is an awkward silence again, so I turn to look at the mourners and see the beach filled with a multitude of angels standing by or just above their people. Some are hovering and it's a sight to behold. A luminous veil of love surrounds them. If the mourners only knew who walked beside them, their fears would lessen.

I turn back to Klaus and his magnificent angel, Kindheart, silently transmits to me words of thankfulness. Klaus standing here is a small improvement. It is a sign from above.

"I'd like to talk to that young man who saw my dog's and cat's spirits. Is he here?"

"Why yes, let me find Mike and bring him over or would you like to join us down by the others?"

"No, I'll wait here."

I stride back to Justine and Mike and whisper to him. He leaves his family and walks with me to Klaus. Maggie is singing with the High School choir *The Twelfth of Never* Madam Norma's favorite song. Accompanied by Anthony Chen, it is one of the most beautiful songs ever written.

As we return to Klaus, I see his angel leave in a whip of light. "Hello," Mike says to Klaus, extending his hand.

Klaus surprisingly takes it. "I need to know what my Freddy, my Tyrone are trying to tell me. You said they're with me. Are they with me still?"

"Yes," assures Mike, "Always."

"What are they trying to tell me?"

"They're communicating their love to you. They want you to rescue an animal. It doesn't matter dog or cat. You need to be with an animal companion to bring you hope on your final life's journey." Klaus looks stunned, and doesn't speak so Mike continues, "If you ever need to talk Ken knows how to get ahold of me."

"Will they go away then?" Klaus is tearful. Mike says, "No, they'll never leave you and will be waiting when your life here on earth ends. See all these people down on the beach with their dogs? Well, there are many spirits of animals, too. I see them all, the beach is crowded with them."

I want to tell Klaus how the beach is filled with angels, too, but instead I silently watch the two men so different in their being yet so alike for their love of animals. They have formed a bond. "Take Ken with you, Mr. Waxman, he will help you find a good animal match for you. I wish you well. Call if you need me. Goodbye." He turns to leave. Klaus reaches a hand out, "Wait, are my two pals happy?"

"Oh yes, you can be sure of it because they are still near you." Justine's handsome son smiles and leaves and Klaus and I stand together watching him walk away while looking out to the Pacific. The quiet waves bring a most peaceful feeling now sparkling in the noonday sun. Reverend Manuel's words and songs from the others have touched the hearts of all. Jamie Bond takes the urn of ashes and Maggie takes Cookie's and they walk into the quiet waves wading knee deep dispersing them, freeing them into the beauty of the sea. King sits by Miss Marilyn's side saying goodbye to the woman he loved with all his being. But he has Miss Marilyn, Tim, Maggie and Noah to love still. He will see her spirit daily and it will give him great comfort in his years ahead. As the memorial service ends, Reverend Manuel speaks his final words, "Go now, live your life as Madam Norma would with dignity, with hope and with love, helping others along the away."

Everyone begins talking and hugging as the service ends. Her family and close friends will head over a short distance to *Jack's By the Sea*, the lovely restaurant looking out to the ocean that Madam Norma loved. We will have a luncheon in her honor with all her favorite dishes including the apple torte they are famous for. I notice King still sits looking out to sea but Miss Marilyn and Maggie are there, bending down on each side of him with hands around him talking to him. Turning back to Klaus, "Let me know if you would like me to go with you to find a dog or cat."

" Okay, Tuesday?"

"Sure, shall I pick you up or would you like to meet in Mystic Bay? "

"I'd like to meet at Madam Norma's like she wanted me to Tuesday morning if that's okay."

"Splendid. Meet you at nine."

Klaus looks down at the ground, pushing grass back with his shoe.

"Okay," is all he says as he turns to leave towards his car. He didn't try to shake my hand. I'm sure he doesn't trust me. I tried not to glow but sometimes I can't help it. People have told me I have sheen to my skin. As I watch his lost soul walk slowly to his car, his angel appears again smiling and nods at me in appreciation. Klaus turns back, "Thank you." He turns and gets into the Mercedes. His angel goes with him.

I think of Madam Norma and then her spirit appears before me transparent, yet radiant and younger looking. She's holding Cookie. Madam Norma wears a colorful blue dress. She is happy. She blows a kiss to me. Then she is gone. My angel heart aches for a moment, then feels joyful, too, for she is with God and all the angels now. She is with her beloved husband, Joe, and they will soar the heavens in harmony.

When Klaus and I meet what will it be like? I don't know. I only know I will give him my best advice, the heavenly way. We will find a dog or cat. My mind is already whirring thinking of where I will take him to find a rescue; there are so many places.

I turn back towards the sea. So many are leaving toward the parking lot. I nod and say hello to a few I know. I see my angel friends walking together with their loved ones toward *Jack's by the Sea*. I see one hundred angels standing in a row watching them go as they sing in quiet tones. I want to stare forever at each one for their beautiful angel souls glow. They are mesmerizing in their beauty and essence of light. In a burst of light they are gone. Marilyn and Maggie are the only people left on the beach, petting and talking to King. I decide to go to them; my angel intuition knows they need me. "Miss Marilyn and Maggie, it was a most beautiful memorial for Madam Norma. A perfect day and the singing was lovely, Maggie."

"Thank you so much." Maggie's face is full of sadness. Miss

Marilyn turns to me, her face wet with tears. "Can you help us get King to go with us to the restaurant? He won't budge."

"Of course, Good King," I touch his head with my hand and a small amount of angel dust sprinkles forth, calming and soothing his mind. Of course Miss Marilyn and Maggie can't tell what I've done. He starts to walk. "Thank you," says Maggie. "You have such a calming way. He misses both GG and Cookie."

"But look, he'll be alright now," says Miss Marilyn wiping her tears. "Come King; let's take this angel of a man, Ken, with us for some good food." I walk with the three of them. Noah and Tim are waiting at the front door of the restaurant with Mabel and her two children. Sea birds call, the sun shines down spreading the warmth and joy that only love can bring. Miss Marilyn called me an angel of a man! That's what I am, I guess. I'm last going into the restaurant and I take a seat among the many tables set for the occasion. King is by the family at the next table. We look at each other. He transmits a message to me. "I know," I say quietly with my mind, "I know King, I miss her, too."

Chapter 17

We Are Their Guardians

It's Tuesday and I wait for Klaus at Madam Norma's front door. King stands beside me. No one is there but Mabel and me. She has set out tea for Klaus and me and is cleaning upstairs. He arrives looking a little better than I thought. His hair is neatly cut and he's wearing a nice polo shirt. "Hello, Klaus," I say walking down the steps to greet him. He doesn't offer his hand and so I don't either. King gives him a happy greeting and Klaus bends down to pet him. " Oh King, good boy, good boy."

He stands and so I start, "Shall we have some tea first before we look for some rescue places nearby?"

"Yes." Klaus looks sad to me as he walks up the steps and into Madam Norma's inviting home. It's warm this October morning, not a cloud in the sky. "Shall we sit outside? Mabel has the tea already simmering and on a warmer."

"Okay." Klaus and King follow me through the kitchen as I place the pot on the tray and proceed out the door. The chairs and flowered glider beckon us to sit under the giant Bishop Pine. For a few minutes I pour tea and admire the lush flowers and bushes of the home. The gardener has taken such care of it that Madam Norma's lovely garden has been featured in many a magazine and on garden club tours in northern California.

I take a sip and each of us takes some pumpkin bread. "First, Klaus, I have contacted Andy Walin, the Mayor's son. He and his wife have an animal rescue in their home sponsored by The Angel

Vibe Association. They find homes in Mystic Bay and Riverton for strays and unwanted dogs and cats. It's behind their home and they only ask for donations. All animals have been spayed and neutered before adopting. Their kennels are full and they have some nice dogs and cats to show us first. Then if none of the dogs or cats matches what you've envisioned, we can drive up north to Millersville and visit a branch of the Humane Society there. It could be a long day or short day depending on what you find."

Klaus nods so I say, "It's hard to be here without her isn't it? "

"Why do you want to help me? You and the Delaney family all seem to hate me underneath your friendliness with everyone else."

Taken aback, I attempt to regain composure. "Hate is such a horrible word, Klaus. No one hates you not the Delaney's and especially not me. I want to help if I can and Madam Norma thought I could help you in many ways." I wait but he doesn't react. He just stares around the garden for a minute. Madam Norma appears to me with lightness in a flowing yellow dress. She holds her beloved Cookie again. She smiles at me, then looks at King, transmitting thoughts. King gets up from the ground and walks over to Klaus and places his head on Klaus' knee. Klaus looks at me surprised. I look up but Madam Norma is gone. Klaus places his hand on King's head. I see him relax. I send angel wind to calm Klaus at this moment. "Can we go when we've finished drinking our tea?"

"Of course." Klaus pets King as King gives him his paw. Above the Bishop Pine Kindheart appears. He takes something from his hand. Is he going to sprinkle angel dust? No, he's sprinkling white feathers. They fall down like a few drops of rain on a sunny day. Klaus is looking up. The look on his face is one of wonder. The feathers stop falling and Kindheart is gone. I say nothing, waiting for Klaus' reaction.

"Did you do that somehow?" Klaus is serious.

"No, Klaus, I'm not that talented. It's a sign; sometimes the angels send us signs. Yours may be feathers. How marvelous for you on the day we're looking for an animal companion for you!"

There is silence between us on the short ride to Andy's home on Meadowbrook. We get out of my car without speaking, either. I knock on the door of the large ranch house. Andy Walin, a gentle soul with a love for animals, greets us with a smile. I introduce him to Klaus and Andy knows of Klaus' actions at the angel debate. However, I explained to him on the phone how Klaus is in need of an animal companion now as he is moving on to make positive changes in his life. Andy is kind and shows us the guesthouse in the back of the property near the flowing stream. There is a large dog run and cat area. The dogs and cats live in the house, which has been set up like a kennel of sorts although there is a large space in the kitchen with a nook and pet beds.

"We have dinner at the kitchen table here. We're home each night. During the day my wife, Mary Jo, takes care of them taking them for individual walks or placing them out to the pen area. We get really attached, as you can tell. We have three dogs and a cat of our own in our house, all rescues." He laughs and I do, too, but Klaus is stone faced. "We actually couldn't stand to see them not adopted, so we just keep them with us until someone comes along, "admits Andy.

"Andy, how nice of you to take this on in addition to your job running the hardware store." I turn toward Klaus. "Andy's father is the Mayor of Mystic Bay. I think you've met him."

"Yes, at the angel debate." I can tell Klaus is looking at the guesthouse in anticipation.

"You know, Mr. Waxman, Ken here told me you wanted a dog or a cat because you lost yours a long time ago."

"Yes, that's correct." Klaus still seems so down I can hardly stand to watch him.

"Well, actually, or shall I say amazingly, we have a dog and cat that came together last week. Their owner, an older man, died suddenly and the family didn't want the animals. If it's a match it would be good for them to be kept together."

Another match made in heaven, I think watching Klaus. I'm wondering if Madam Norma's spirit has anything to do with this.

Klaus' face is one of shock. "Really, yes, I'd like to see them first." I knew in my heart that Klaus would take the first animal he saw. Andy told me about these two but I only could hope. Now as I watch Andy go get the two and bring them outside to us I find myself joyful in anticipation. Klaus is looking more positive too. The door opens and out a big Golden Retriever bounds. Andy carries a black cat with white spots. "This Golden is Lucky and this is Dot the cat. They are best pals for sure."

Klaus drops to his knees with hands outstretched. Lucky runs to Klaus's arms and as Andy sets Dot down, the cat runs to him, too. Yes, I transmit wordlessly to Kindheart who's standing near. A heavenly match it is!

After Klaus has stayed awhile in the kitchen petting the animals, Andy goes over the health records. He has Klaus sign all the necessary paperwork. Klaus' expression has changed as he hands the check and looks at his new companions. He is anxious to get them home. He says thank you and shakes Andy's hand. He doesn't offer his hand to me and I decide to wait until next time to put out my hand to him. He does say thank you to me as we finish putting the animals in his car. He waves as he drives away with his new animals. I feel a big glow coming on. I couldn't stop smiling myself as I thanked Andy again. "Ken, I am sure these animals will be loved. I am grateful to you for bringing him here. "

I drive back home and park the car in my driveway. I walk over to *The Painted Butterfly*. Justine is helping a customer. An easel is set up in the window. She's decided to paint on Saturday afternoons sitting in the window so the public can watch her work. She's going to start this coming Saturday, which is Halloween and there's a street fair. Shopkeepers will be displaying items on sale for fall before Christmas wares are set out the following week. She's going to show the kid's art too. I'll have a table full of angel items to sell. I look around at the cheerfully decorated store all butterflies. It mirrors my own store. We think alike, Justine and I with our comfy couches and chairs. Cookies and water are on the table to share.

Her demeanor has changed these last few months. I notice she looks more radiant then ever in a pink sweater and jeans. Her hair is pulled back. Her smile is infectious today. When the customer leaves she looks at me and I am silent for a moment. "How did it go with Klaus? He found both a dog and a cat?"

"Yes. It was another miracle, Justine. Andy had a dog and cat that were left there after their owner died last week. Klaus didn't say anything at first. He knelt down and they ran to him. All he said then was, "I'd like to take them both. I'd like to take them to their new home." Andy only requires a small donation but Klaus wrote him a big check. It was a wonderful thing to witness. He left and I knew a change had happened that moment, a change for the good."

~~~~~~~~~~

The Halloween Street Fair is always a success. Our seaside town is in full of Halloween and fall decorations on sale. The morning is cool, but the sun starts shining as the fog clears. The men from The San Francisco Shakers are handling all the sports programs today and I'm helping set up the angel gifts outside the store. Val is with Spencer at the sports program but he'll be back at noon to help me. He will love it. He and Spencer can tour around with January going from store to store. Storeowners have apple cider and cookies and other snacks to share with the public outside their stores. The town is hosting a big Halloween party for kids at the High School gym at five o'clock.

I walk over to *The Painted Butterfly* to see Justine sitting in the window painting away. She's creating a purple butterfly with little
~~~~~~~~~~

flowers around it. Her white dress reminds me of the most beautiful angel I ever saw. Her eyes have a sense of fun. People are starting to gather. Two other paintings are displayed in the large window. One is of a black pug with a yellow butterfly on his nose. The other painting is of an orange cat sitting on a shocking pink chair. His tail has a silver butterfly lighting on the tail's tip. Both are precious. The children's paintings are displayed as well. One is Billie Jo's. She's painted Sadie sitting with pink angel wings at her shoulders. The other is Val's. It's his rendition of Barty lying in his dog bed with a butterfly on his nose too. Justine looks up, and smiles at me. I wave and go back to my own store. It's a good day for the town. I haven't heard from Klaus. I decide to wait until Monday night to call to see if he still wants to meet at Madam Norma's on Tuesday morning. Justine thinks he will but I'm not sure. As if on cue my cell rings. It's Klaus. "I would like to meet but I have a court case to deal with. It might be a few weeks before we could meet. Would that be all right to keep our appointment?"

"Of course," I tell him. "Give me a call when you can." My angel heart beats a big thump. I breathe in an angel breath. A change has come. It's never to late for change. But Klaus didn't say anything about Lucky and Dot and I forgot to ask. Will he follow through? When I tell Justine what Klaus said to me her positive reaction gives me hope. "The word 'time' comes to me, Ken. He will call you but it may be awhile. He's processing everything that's happened. Klaus needs the healing of time."

Chapter 18

Star Dust

We've just come home from a wonderful Monday after Thanksgiving. Everyone was at Pam Ellen and Bob's. They invited January, July, Spencer and Heather as well as Angie and Ricky. The food was heavenly. Not hearing from Klaus nagged me as we played games and watched football. It's been almost a month and no call. Shall I call him? I don't want to bother him. I'm helping Angie and Ricky put up the Christmas trees in the store. I have so many angel ornaments to sell although actually I hate parting with any one of them.

Angie asks me, "Have you heard from Mr. Waxman and how Lucky and Dot are doing?" Angie is concerned for the animals. She volunteers for Andy in her spare time and takes photos of the animals for their newsletter. "Andy asked me to ask you."

" No," I shake my head. "But you've just helped me. I'm going to call him on his cell and leave a message if he's not home." To my surprise he answers.

"Klaus Waxman, hello Ken." He sounds pretty good.

"Klaus I just called because I haven't heard from you. I'm hoping you want to meet with me on Tuesday, tomorrow, if you're free?"

There is hesitation and then, "Yes, I was going to call you but I've been so busy with work and Lucky and Dot. I have a sitter for them during the day. Yes, I can meet you at Madam Norma's. Nine, tomorrow?"

"Yes, Thank you. I'll see you then." When I hang up, I realize I'm looking forward to Tuesday with Klaus and our conversation. Mabel enjoys making tea for us I know and I believe she is also comforted by my presence when I stop by. With a heavy heart, I think of Madam Norma and how life for her family and the town has changed and must go on without her. The sign outside her house that still reads *Madam Norma's Parlor* will remain for years now. Dan Pico wrote an article about her in *The San Francisco Chronicle* on how she impacted many a life here. Yet, her spirit will always be present with love and good wishes for us all. She will appear to me from beyond as she already has a few times now. I will treasure the thought of seeing her.

I've invited everyone over to my house for pizza tonight, as we are tired of leftovers. Pam Ellen, Bob and Bobby aren't here yet and I'm watching from the kitchen window as the children play in the yard with the dogs. I feel the warm connection of friendship between Mac and Justine as they sit in the garden talking. I have an angel's ear and so I am able to listen in on their conversation but I never have. I can hear them as clearly as if standing beside them. This time I wipe my hands and decide to go to the open back door.

The sky is a robin's egg blue mixed with the fluffiest of clouds I've seen ever. The roses sway sharing their fragrant beauty with the peaceful scene. It lightens my angel heart. I instantly send butterflies into the yard with my hands outstretched. On the angel wind fly butterflies of various sizes and colors. The butterflies swirl towards Mac and Justine circling around them. The two of them stop their talking and begin laughing. The largest one lights on Mac's shoulder, then flies away as quickly as it came.

As the children see the butterflies fly towards them now they squeal with delight holding out their hands. "This is incredible," Mac says looking at Justine.

"They only come on the sweetest of days," Justine tells him with a light shining in her blue eyes.

"Can I ask you a question?" Mac says shyly. Justine shakes her head yes. She may have known what he was going to ask. "Would you go out with me on a real date? Dinner some night, just the two of us?" Embarrassed, he turns his head towards the children now watching as they chase the butterflies off to the back near the fence. Mac waits a moment anticipating her response.

"Why, yes Mac, to answer your question of course, yes!" Mac stands up and takes her hand in his. She stands, smiling at him.

Billie Jo comes up to them and hugs both. "Why do they come, Justine? Do you know why the butterflies are around you all the time? You paint them and now they're coming around us!"

" I think the angels must have sent butterflies to remind us how love is swirling all around us, Billie Jo." She turns to look at Mac as he bends down to look eye level at his granddaughter.

"Just like we love you, Billie Jo." Mac hugs her.

Val runs up to them and I walk out the door. He sees me and shouts, "Wow Dad, those butterflies are so pretty! They landed on our fingers for just a second!"

As they all turn to look at me, I want to tell them how we angels live as humans here and how everyone and everything is made of stardust like the earth and the moon. I want to tell them how I love living as an ordinary man with a son in the quaint and lovely town of Mystic Bay. I want to tell them so much about life and the stars and flying at night when no one can see on the most beautiful blue planet in the Milky Way. If I could only share what angels know best that only kindness matters and love is the heart and soul of the earth.

Instantly Ned's spirit is smiling by the roses at us, then he is gone like the flicker of a candle blown out in the breeze. He knows Mac has fallen in love with Justine and wants to care for her and the children until his time to leave the Earth Realm, a long time from now. Speechless, I take in the peacefulness of the scene as the words come to Justine as natural as her sensitive spirit.

Looking down at the innocent children's faces, she says, "The angels sent me the most beautiful gift."

Val asks, "The butterflies?"

"Yes, of course, but most especially the gift of you two and your fathers. I needed to be with you all. It's made me so very happy."

The butterflies appear again swirling around us. Not by magic but with angel wind they land on Val and Billie Jo's shoulders. The children freeze for a moment then the butterflies fly away fluttering their goodbye.

I say, "Angels came to town last year for the children to see them so the world would learn their message of love and hope. Love brings us only the good things in life. Love comes on the wings of butterflies and angels."

I hear a choir of angels singing joyously in the heavens. In the endless infinity of heaven, stars are born and planets, moons and solar systems and millions of galaxies fill the night skies with their beauty. I thank Him who made it all. Val and I hold hands now. The late fall afternoon sun starts it's descent.

Chapter 19

A Rainy Day Can Wash His Sorrow Away

Klaus and I have talked for eight weeks of Tuesdays now at Madam Norma's home on Moon Road. Mabel has provided us with tea and fruit breads and left us alone so she can do her busy work in the house. Miss Marilyn and Tim are at their store on Tuesday mornings, so we get our time to ourselves in the cozy parlor or outside in the beauty of the garden. The faithful companionship of King comforts us both. We are greeted with barks of love as we enter the home.

As we've chatted, our first sessions are about Lucky and Dot and how it feels having animals to love again. He still has not spoken much to Miranda but he has put limits on her spending. He agrees to work with a psychologist. He's also started AA and has a sponsor he is beginning to trust.

"I don't feel like having a drink when I get home any longer or stopping at *DiMaggio's Place*. Taking care of Lucky and Dot, well, it's my top priority now."

Yes, through tea and conversation and Madam Norma's warm home, Mabel's care, and King's enduring presence, we have formed a bond. I knew he was beginning to trust me when his story opened up like a dam bursting down a river. I've learned a great deal about Klaus. And with the help of Kindheart always standing near, I have seen the memories of Klaus' childhood as Kindheart extends his hands forming a mist to the side of Klaus for me to witness. Just as the mist showed me memories of Justine and the butterflies, I see Klaus' life through veiled light. I see his life

123

torn apart by sorrow, reminiscent of so many kids, including some of the sad stories of the football players I've worked with. The misty remembering's of long ago…. *A poor six-year-old Klaus appears in ragged clothes. He sits crying on the stoop of his house in a small Kansas town. His punitive grandmother is raising him. After his mother died and father left he had nowhere else to go. Her mean face is yelling at him. "Play with the dog next door cuz we can't afford no dog, you good for nothin!"*

The mist clears as Klaus tells me, "My father came to see me at school to say goodbye. He might have come back to town to get me but I was afraid to go outside. The principal tried to encourage me, but I wouldn't go. My grandmother told me so many lies about him. It's my biggest regret." Through the misty memory I see…

Klaus sits in school, his safe place. His love of school helps him cope, he tells me. It is the only part of his life that was good. I see him helping neighbors with their chores and earning money for clothes and extra food. I see him in high school and with his teachers encouragement, he excels. I see him at seventeen, at the dusty bus stop with a small suitcase in hand, having graduated early to go to Kansas State on a full scholarship. He doesn't look back at the small town as he finds a seat and the bus moves forward. His new life is starting. I see tears fall as he looks out through the bus drivers' window, looking ahead, vowing never to look back at the horrid life he came from.

The mist leaves the room and as our sessions continue he tells me when he started college, his life was beginning to look promising. During his undergrad days, he took in Freddy and Tyrone, from a fellow student who didn't want them anymore. They were throwaways and became his family, his pals. For eight years they were with him in his tiny apartment as he went on to grad school. Sadly, they both died during his last year. He pushed on through grief, became a lawyer and worked in Kansas City that's where he met Sally. She was so beautiful, almost perfection to look at. She captivated him. She claimed her childhood was akin to his. As we talk during the sessions he comes to see her as a manipulative woman only wanting money. She left him for a wealthy lawyer he knew. He realizes now how similar she was in personality to his grandmother and eventually to his daughter. Sally left him with the baby, Miranda. As he worked hard at his career, he found he hired babysitter after babysitter. He was too engrossed in his career and making money to pay attention to what was happening. He started drinking, spoiling the child. Her manipulative tendencies were almost unbearable. He didn't know how to stop her behavior when he heard about Bobby's breakup with Miranda. Klaus became unglued.

"I was afraid of her. No one has broken up with Miranda before. She's always in control of every relationship, especially with me, her own father! I realize now I had to be in control trying to help Miranda punish Bobby. How could I have been so wrong? My drinking didn't help. I was drunk everyday, yelling at work too."

We've talked on Tuesdays with honesty, although not mentioning angels much. His angel, Kindheart, always is in the room with us. I glance at his powerful presence this eighth session now as King does. Madam Norma's spirit comes for a moment. King follows her silent instruction and lays his head on Klaus' lap. With his heavy heart, Klaus automatically pets his head. "Good boy, King," he says.

On this rainy January morning I ask him, "What do you want your legacy to be, Klaus?" His reply is what I've been waiting for.

" Well, I would like to ask you to help me to be someone who is remembered for improving my life. I want to be forgiven by those I've hurt like the people who work for me. I want to ask Bobby and his family to forgive me, too. I need you to tell me what to say. And most of all, I want to finally talk about angels. I need it Ken, I really do. I want learning about angels to be part of my legacy too."

Tears form in my eyes. I have kept Klaus and my meetings to myself although the other angels probably have guessed by now. Justine's psychic ways may have figured it out too but what Klaus has told me has stayed within the walls of this room. These moments are just between the two of us. So with Mabel's nurturing tea, and King's devotion, I say, "I am pleased, Klaus. You have made great progress. Yes, let's talk of angels and forgiveness and how to go about achieving that."

We make a plan for me to call Bobby and arrange to get together. Klaus will have an office meeting set up towards the end of the week also. He wants me to be at both meetings and I will do as he asks. So as the rain streams down the windows in the parlor and King curls at Klaus' feet, I speak the words so necessary for him to hear.

"I believe we all have a guardian angel and yours is always near. You have free will Klaus, yes, but your angel and other angels are there for you to ask for help. Ask them out loud, ask them anything and words and answers will come to your mind."

Klaus looks doubtful for a moment. "All those angels stories and sightings from the debate; you actually believe they are true?"

"Yes, I believe they are. So many miracles have happened here in Mystic Bay. Don't you see you are one of those miracles?"

Klaus glances out the window. The only sound we hear is the rain as it falls pitter patting down the panes and that of the occasional car with tires splashing down the street. For a minute or so we hear Mabel cleaning upstairs. We turn at the same time admiring King dreaming peaceful dreams now. Kindheart glows behind Klaus' chair and I am awestruck by his angelic beauty and energy. Then Klaus speaks.

"All these weeks I've gone home after our sessions and thought about the stories at the debate. I want to believe the little children really saw angels and Benny played the magical song the angels sang for him. I want to believe, Ken, but then I get afraid it's not true. I'm afraid the promise of angels is all a dream. Nothing ever worked out for me. Look at the mess my life is. Look at Miranda and what indulging her has done?" He bows his head and King gets up to stretch. Wandering over to him, he puts his head on Klaus' lap again. Shaking away some of his sorrow now, Klaus smiles petting him again.

"You see Klaus, there is the sign that it's not a dream. You have your animals to love now and to help you through. You will be forgiven, I'm sure by the Delany's. You go home to your pets love and now you are figuring out how to handle your problems with Miranda. You are feeling the angels and God's love more and more each day. Believe it for it is real and try to forgive yourself. It is so very important."

"Madam Norma said you see angels. Do you see mine?"

"At times, yes, I think I feel your angels presence." I move some angel wind toward Klaus and he takes in a deep breath. He takes a sip of tea and looks again out the window. The rain is coming harder now but I see his mind churning. "It's a beginning, a new life for me. I feel it, Ken. I don't feel anger down in my soul anymore." Klaus turns to me and I nod with a smile. Kindheart and I look at each other. "Amen," he says to me in an angel's whisper.

Chapter 20

There Is Light In Forgiveness

The sun is still in the sky when we get to *The Painted Butterfly* on Saturday evening. Bobby, Justine, Pam Ellen and Bob are there waiting. What doesn't surprise me at all is how kind they are to the man who tried to hurt their business with his bizarre store and accusations. Klaus is also surprising me, saying words I will never forget, words that ring the bell of forgiveness.

"I am trying to change my life with Ken's help, and AA. I hope you can find it in your hearts to forgive me for the unkind way I treated you all. I am truly sorry. It will never happen again."

Bobby, as the spokesman for the family says, " Klaus, we already have. We said before that we wish you well always and we meant it." That was all. Everyone shook hands and Klaus and I plan to have dinner at Mahoney's. Klaus waits outside and Justine says quietly, "You have done an amazing job with him."

"All I do is listen, mostly. The angels do the rest. Klaus realizes so much on his own."

"Never taking credit as usual. He's evolving and you have had a big part in that. Someday, I want to ride on your coat tails to heaven, Ken." She hugs me. " Mac and I are taking the kids for pizza. They'll be at Mac's when you get home, no rush. We're going to play a game or two and Barty will be with us. Maybe Val could spend the night with me. I'd like it if he could?"

"Sure, how great, ask him."

If he agrees then I can fly with my friends tonight. The seven of us can soar together. It's been a few months now since we've all been together flying. I say goodbye to the family with thankfulness. Klaus appears relieved as we walk to the restaurant near Main Street. It's a cold night and all the blossoms of geraniums in the hanging baskets are brilliant pinks and reds, but they are in need of warmth. It soothes my angel soul as I send angel wind and they stretch in the warmth.

We eat corned beef sandwiches with Russian dressing and drink iced tea in the Irish themed restaurant. We see some people I know and I introduce him. Some had been at the debate but they are polite and kind of surprised to see Klaus and I together, I'm guessing. When we are finished and alone Klaus says, "Nobody said anything unkind to me."

"This is a pretty terrific town. People are nice."

As we are about to leave, the other six angels walk in and I beckon them over to join us instead of sitting at another table. We exchange pleasantries and they order and Klaus and I order some dessert. Klaus, the former creator of such havoc, is totally unaware he is sitting with seven angels living as humans in Mystic Bay. Each of us is praying for him and sending him angel wind. I must say I am surprised when he tells them about his apology to Bobby and family. He asks us what else he could do to make it up to the town. Taylor says, "You'll find a way. Something will come to you." Gabe adds, "Yes, it's really great you're thinking this way, Klaus, it really is."

Klaus says, " I thought I'd write a letter to the town and explain how I've done a lot of thinking and changing."

The seven us agree that would be really nice. We eat and talk about other things. Klaus watches us. They ask him about his law firm and he tells us they practice general law. Then surprisingly he describes his story, the story he's told me. From a poor childhood he told them of the change in his life, getting scholarships to undergrad and law school. He obviously has pushed to have a better life like *The Little Engine That Could*. With the woman he loved, he felt he was unstoppable. But then she left, and he was left to raise Miranda. She never really grew up.

He tells us of his regrets. The angels glow and feel his pain as I do. It's like he'd been waiting to spill the sadness his whole life. Unknowingly, now, he has done so before angels.

We don't give advice. We just listen. Gabe encourages him to come to a parenting meeting once a week that he leads with Reverend Manual. Klaus accepts, and we send angel wind to him.

July begins telling us the news about the new episode of her TV show that will be live again from Town Square in a few months. Writer Noah Greenstreet is shooting a documentary on the town and July's show will be part of the documentary. People that have had sightings will be interviewed. There will be singing and displays of the angel artwork the little boy drew on the Jumbotron again. It will be a history of what's happened in the town since the book, *My California Angel*, came out hinting Hannah and Gabe were angels. The show will tell how Hannah wrote the book *Town With the Angel Vibe*. Subsequently, all the volunteerism and love poured out of the town.

Although I can tell that Gabe is a little nervous about it all, I'm sure it will be well done. Noah and his wife, Maggie, Madam Norma's great granddaughter, saw us angels fly a few years back. She remembers it now as only a dream.

"It sounds wonderful," Klaus says with sincerity. All of us glance at each other. I think I see a faint smile come to his lips as he feels the warmth of friendship from us.

When I get home, Barty is there to greet me. Justine had texted she sensed Barty wanted to stay home. "Interesting for me to get a wordless message from Barty," she wrote. So, I do something I haven't done since he was a pup. I have an urge to pick him up and stand on the front porch. No one is stirring on the street. Mac and Billie Jo are asleep. So are Justine and Val at her house. My wings spread three feet on either side of me. They shine in the foggy night and I glow.

Surprised at my impulsivity, "You want a ride like the night I found you? Okay, my little man, let's fly."

Although Barty weighs twenty pounds he fits just fine in my big arms. I lift off feeling the euphoria of freedom. Barty amazes me flying. It's as if it's second nature to him. He's not frightened. I'm holding him just as I held him before that night years ago. He feels secure and I transmit to him with angel wind and kindness to close his eyes and rest. But I notice him looking down with curiosity. Barty transmits wordlessly through pictures he sends me in his mind to fly above the rooftops of town out to the bucolic hills, farms and ranches on the outskirts of Mystic Bay.

Over Doc Lindley's farm we go watching the sheep and deer below as they sleep in the pasture and near the barn. Doc Lindley is on his front porch. I can barely see his face in the porch light. The old rescued dog is at his feet. Knowing he can't see me, I wonder if Doc can see Barty in my arms, but he doesn't glance our way. No, he is looking at the night, breathing it in the way most humans do with awe and wonder. Of course, the old dog sees us. Dogs always do.

Barty and I sail above the trees and streams. I see Bobby's new house and know he's sleeping peacefully now with his new additions, his three rescue dogs. I wish him love to find a mate he so desperately wants and needs. I sigh as I fly looking up at the sky above. It's deep indigo and misty. I am just about ready to fly us back home.

Suddenly, Barty sends thoughts to me. I know then I must fly fast towards Riverton and the lonely curve in the road where I helped Cliff James that day so long ago. Barty barks letting me know to stop and fly to the ground. I slow down touching the ground lightly. It's there we see her, an injured dog, lying at the side of the road just as I found Barty on that rain-soaked street in

San Francisco.

Worried, I wonder how I can pick her up and take her to Doc Josh with Barty in my arms, I use my angel mind and call out for Doc Josh for help. It's dark but my angel night vision has kicked in. The dog is small and has been hit by a car, but breathing and awake. She seems to know I'm there to help. I send her angel wind to calm her. Barty licks the wounded dog, then sits besides her.

There is no collar on the furry dog. I'm guessing some soulless individual, leaving her to perish on the dangerous road, has dropped her off. Tonight there are no cars in sight. It's only a matter of ten minutes before Josh has flown to us. Without words he uses his healing angel dust, waving it over the dog to calm her and to heal what hurts until he gets her back to his office. He nods at me, picks the dog up in his steady hands and lifts away with silvery wings into the misty night. Barty almost flies back into my arms. We set off for home back over the meadows that smell of crops and the animals on the farmland. We get to Doc Lindley's farm. I look down but he has gone in. His porch light still glows and I feel love for the man who has rescued or saved so many animals in his career and now has his most important work. His deer farm has given a new life to those forgotten ones.

I know in my angel heart that the dog we found tonight will come to live with us. It's as if Barty sensed her and knew we would fly to find her. "Well done, Barty," I say as we fly towards home awaiting well-earned rest. "Won't Val be surprised?"

Chapter 21

The Letter and Madam Norma's Vision

I rose early this morning to read the letter Madam Norma wrote to me and mailed before she died. It read, "Do not open til June 23rd." I store it in my bureau drawer. I've been tempted to read it so many times but I knew she had reason for asking that I wait these long months. It's the day before the July North TV show; however, there's a special event I must attend today. Val is still asleep and so I sit on the bed, Barty and Honey, our rescue dog, are both with Val. Honey gets to sleep on the bed. The little fur ball has been with us only a few months and has taken to us as we have to her.

I open the letter and it is with tears that I read:

My dearest Ken,

I had a vision today, a vision about you and the ones you love so dearly. Today when you open this letter, June 23rd, you will attend the wedding of Justine and Mac in my garden. You have brought them together and they will be happy. You do so much for others, I know. Val has a new life, as does Billie Jo because of you. But, there is more.

Today as their wedding concludes you will find the new bee species that Dr. Xander Sing, the Entomologist, is looking for. You will find the hive with sheer angel sense.

I wish you a wonderful life here. And before I forget, I know that you have also changed one other life. Klaus Waxman will surprise you with his newfound soul. You have been my dear friend. *I'll be*

135

seeing you again in Heaven's Realm.

Love Always,

Madam Norma

Tears stream down my face as I hold the letter to my heart. This woman had a gift like no other. I get up and take the letter to my drawer and put it underneath my t-shirts. I start to dress unable to think of anything else. Then Val walks in the room. "I'm taking the dogs out, Dad, but will you help me with my tie in a minute?" Before I can answer, he's bounding down the steps with dogs in tow. Happiness is his nature now.

~~~~~~~~~~

It's a glorious summer day as Justine and Mac take their vows. Justine looks ever so lovely in the street length off white silk dress and blue suede heels. Billie Jo is wearing a yellow dress with a blue sash and shoes. All the men in the family including Val are wearing khaki's, blue shirts and yellow ties with blue polka dots. Justine and Billie Jo carry small bouquets of white and yellow roses. Madam Norma's family is here as well as Laurjean. Also, Donnie and their sons are in attendance. Just the closest family and friends attend.

The couple kisses and every one cheers in the most beautiful jeweled garden in Mystic Bay. The sun shines as they all walk down Moon Road towards *Jack's By the Sea* where we will feast and toast the afternoon away. But I stay back for a moment. I tell Bobby to take Val and not wait for me. I have something to do. I'm alone with King in the back yard. The Bishop Pine sways and I try to use the angel sense that Norma said would find the bee's hive. Then it comes to me. I will listen with my angel ear for the sound. I will ask all angels to help me for this honey bee will help the world's bee population in their work toward saving the earth.

I hear it, a slight buzz coming from the owl house atop the roof. King hears it, too. I quickly go to the garage and get the old ladder. I take off my jacket and climb the ladder to the owl house. There
~~~~~~~~~~

the hive is under the eave of the owl's nesting place. The bees with the golden wings are buzzing but seem to be fine with my presence. I think no owl is inside. Then in a swish an owl comes out and I fall back but onto the Bishop Pine's trunk, finding the wise steady tree and limbs steadying me. I take out the cell phone and carefully snap a photo for Dr. Xander Sing. I climb back down, and call Dr. Sing. He answers immediately as he has been here over a year and a half having sightings but not finding any live hives. When I tell him the news, he drops his phone." I'll be right there," he says.

When Dr. Sing arrives with his team a few minutes later, I am ready to show him. "There might be an owl in there." As he climbs down the ladder after taking photographs I tell him I must be anonymous for Madam Norma's spirit sent me a sign, a prediction of where to look in a letter not to be opened until this very day. Ever grateful, we shake hands. I put King in the house and tell him wordlessly that Tim, Marilyn, Maggie, Noah and Mabel will be right back. He looks at me, knowing I'm an angel with his animal's acute understanding. I hug him goodbye.

I walk in *Jack's by the Sea* with a smile on my face. Happiness is on everyone else's faces. They are eating lunch on the patio, feeling the salty warm breeze and the sun shining. As we finish and the red velvet wedding cake is passed around, Mac stands.

"I thank you all my wonderful new friends and family, for being so welcoming to me and Billie Jo. I toast my new family, Liz, Mike, Pam Ellen, Bob and Bobby and you my friends who our extended family. And to you my lovely wife, Justine, well, an angel must have sent you!"

Chapter 22

Town of Angels

July North, the USA's favorite TV host and resident angel, walks up the steps to the gazebo on Mystic Bay's large Town Square. Her face is glowing from happiness. It's a big day in town. Noah Greenstreet is shooting part of his documentary called *Town of Angels* and July's TV Show will be a part of it. Her sparkling angel earrings set off her swept up dark hair. We angels sit in the first few rows around the gazebo as well as everyone else who can crowd in. We're sitting on blankets and chairs. There are young and old and in between. Dogs and babies sit on laps or on blankets. There are psychics like Justine, Pam Ellen, Liz and Mike and also other ordinary town folk in the audience embracing this day. All is good in the *Town of Angels*.

The town's clock tower has struck ten as July begins on this sunny summer day. "Welcome welcome everyone," she says cheerily while sitting on one of the white whicker chairs set up for the show. A large bandstand is to her left where the San Francisco Symphony is waiting to play and giant Jumbotrons hang on the town's tallest building so even more can watch from the storefronts and windows in town.

"We are so fortunate to be among the kindly residents of Mystic Bay, California as well as its friends and neighbors. We will showcase not only the wonderful things happening in Mystic Bay but in our sister town to the south, Riverton. We will also introduce you, our audience, to the many fortunate people who live in these parts who have had angel experiences. I will interview them along

139

with author, Noah Greenstreet, who is here today to begin the shooting of his documentary about the town. He is calling it, *Town of Angels*.

As you know this town is known for it's volunteerism and welcoming atmosphere. One of our town's residents, Hannah O'Ryan Ryder, wrote a book a few years back about the town called *Town with the Angel Vibe*. Hannah came on my first two shows here. The next year our TV show showcased the angel sightings in town *Songfest For the Angels*. Come on up, Noah and Hannah!"

As the lovely Hannah, Gabe's half-angel daughter and Josh's wife comes up on stage, her red haired beauty and confidence strike me. She and handsome Noah sit down and July welcomes them again. July begins with Hannah asking her how the angel like attitude came about in the misty seaside and tourist-loving town of Mystic Bay.

"After the novel was written about me, insinuating I was an angel swarms of TV reporters swept into town. It was a circus-like-atmosphere and I was fearful and refused to be interviewed. But then you came to town with your show, July and interviewed me with such kindness and understanding. "

"Hannah, it was a pleasure to meet you then and get to know you as a friend. It was a hard time for you. Please tell us then what happened."

"I explained to the viewers that I am just a woman from the town of Mystic Bay who had written stories for my college class. My professor used those ideas to write the novel."

"Yes, he apologized on our show." I note neither of them named Sam Blakley. Why give the guy more publicity than he already has had? And Hannah is not technically lying, for she is only half angel. If someone had asked her outright then she would have had to comply by telling the truth. A little angel dust must have been wafting in the air. Hannah speaks of the town's kindness to her through the ordeal, how no one would talk to the reporters and how in the immediate aftermath, volunteerism ensued.

The town's kind people set out not only to protect Hannah from the onslaught of media but for a few years now they have been doing kind deeds, helping others and fostering and adopting children and rescuing animals. Thus, she wrote her own book and July had a wonderful show in town again talking about the changes the town had made.

Then July turns to Noah. "Please tell us why you are shooting this documentary, Noah."

"Well, I believe as do many others, the world needs to hear these stories first hand. Yes, children saw angels first, but adults have had sightings also. I feel as a writer that this story will be my most important work. The theme of the documentary will be how a charming seaside town known for its psychics became the place of angel sightings. It is extraordinary what's happened here. I can't wait to tell this story."

"Noah this is so great. Your late father, Marshall Greenstreet, was a well-known novelist and came to town years ago interviewing psychics. Those interviews inspired him to write his *Connor Diamond Series*. Tell me though, how it happened that you landed here?"

"My father and mother moved here when my mother became ill. They both felt it was such a special town and wanted to return to the seaside Mystic Bay. There was a good atmosphere and the people were kind. My parents have passed away now, but I stayed on to finish writing my father's last book. I fell in love with the town and people. The angel sightings happened, and then I met my lovely wife, and here I am doing a most remarkable thing, a documentary on angels in the town I love."

"Wow, how special, Noah. I am sure your parents would be proud of you. Now we are going to interview your wife Maggie Greenstreet. Come on up, Maggie."

Maggie Greenstreet is an amazing psychic herself, she finally is going to explain her own experiences.

"I have psychic abilities with nature. I can hear the hum of life in plants and trees. On a beautiful spring day, I babysat the little mute girl who saw an angel. But before she saw the angel I suddenly saw the spirit of my beloved dog, Jeb, who had passed away months before. He was standing in the sunlight with a golden glow around him. I took the little girl's hand and walked toward my dog but he disappeared. It was then that she pointed to a fallen bird on the ground. As if someone was lifting it, the bird regained life. It seemed tossed in the air flying away. The little girl said 'angel' and pointed in the sky. This is how the sightings started. This has changed my life."

No one has heard this story before. The audience sits in quiet wonder.

"Go on Maggie, I believe there is more." July knows that angel dust erased Noah and her memory of seeing us angels flying the night of the eclipse of the moon but we would never erase her own angel sighting.

"I met my own guardian angel. I see him only at certain times. I knew him as a human for a while. So the book about Hannah could have had a point. All I know for sure is that angels come as humans at times. I've seen my guardian angel in angel form and in human form. When I sang at your Songfest, he was there. I decided not to keep it in any longer. The world needs to know I've seen my own guardian angel. I have talked to him. He was there when I met Noah as a child and he was there when Noah and I married on the beach. As God is my witness, I have seen an angel."

Noah takes one if Maggie's hands and July takes her other hand. "This is extraordinary," July says. "Everyone, this probably happens all the time. Maybe people don't know they meet actual angels but here we are today with such a compelling story. Thank you, Maggie!"

Val looks up at me with his shining brown eyes. "Dad, this is so cool, Maggie saw an angel and so angels are everywhere, huh, Dad?"

"Yes, my son. I think they are. You and I are lucky to live in this town. I was lucky enough to get to know you and be your dad. It all happened because little kids and adults saw angels." It's like music hearing Val call me 'Dad' now.

"And Billie Jo too, she's lucky Dad?"

"Yes, and Billie Jo, too! "

"And Honey?"

"Yes," I laugh tousling his hair. "And our Honey too and everyone we know."

When the show comes back on the air, July has only Noah Greenstreet sitting next to her. "It's all wonderful, Noah, and now I am going to show the world again the artwork done by a child with disabilities. He says an angel came to him guiding his hand how to draw the masterpieces." On the Jumbotron for the entire world to see once more are the two lovely impressionistic paintings of angels. As if done by Monet long ago they are warmly painted with a palate of pastels. A silence comes over the crowd. Then the applauding, cheering and standing sweeps through us all. Val and I are on our feet!

As the crowd calms July states, "The child is anonymous for obvious reasons and afterward went back to drawing like a child but it was indeed a miracle. It's changed the way many of us have viewed the world. Also, another anonymous child with disabilities spoke for the first time when she saw an angel, as Maggie Greenstreet told us. Her first word was 'angel'. She must remain anonymous too. And now please welcome to the gazebo, Doc Eric Lindley."

Doc Eric Lindley walks up and is given a standing ovation. The only vet in town before Josh arrived; he is well loved and respected. July asks him to please tell us all he knows of angels and the experiences he's had with them.

He explains in detail his help birthing the fawn on his rescue farm. He describes the actual way it happened. "A soft light appeared but I didn't have time to contemplate it because I was struggling with the difficult birth. I couldn't get the fawn out of his mother no matter how hard I tried. I was afraid of losing them both. My strength was leaving me. Miraculously, I felt hands on each arm helping me pull the fawn out. I spoke to the angels. Although, I couldn't see them I knew they were there. I thanked them that night. Over the years I've had similar experiences but none so obvious as this. The angels were definitely with me. My wife and I named the deer, Angel. July, you have her photo."

"Yes, the photo is on the Jumbotron now for the world to see. How lovely Doctor Lindley. What a very special and enlightening story."

"Thank you, July," he replies. There is applause and a wave of peace filling Town Square. July says, "Doc Lindley and Noah, this is a remarkable day for us all and for our next guest. Please come on up, Clifford James."

Cliff sits down in the whicker chair, shaking hands with Doc Lindley and Noah. "Please tell us your own angel sighting, Clifford." So Cliff begins telling the story of how I helped him that night on the dangerous road out of Riverton. He relates how no one was there and suddenly there I was with a tow truck and no visible name to read on my work shirt or on the tow truck. He explains how I made him go in front of the truck. He explains how he didn't see the man fix his truck in an instant. As he's talking, I send angel wind to calm him, as he is appearing nervous. I also send a twinge of soft angel dust. A few angels' sprinkles fall down around him. Only angels and animals can see angel dust. For the moment, he doesn't remember to say my name. He forgets the angel he thinks helped him had looked a lot like me. As he stops for a moment trying to remember, I see his brow furrow, then he goes on with the story. I am grateful for this. Yes, I slowed the cars down so he could get off the road fast. It was my pleasure. That kind of work is what I long for. July thanks him and we go to commercial.

When the show returns, July sits with Noah and the parents of the little girl who saw an angel when she was young. "She rose up at only three years old, raised both hands in the air and said "Gloria Halleluiah!" Of course the little girl, now in her twenties, is not present. Keeping the children anonymous is primary.

Jamie Bond is called up and sits by July, telling a most endearing tale. He talks of Madam Norma, Miss Marilyn and Tim and how they are angels on earth to him helping his life. He believes wholeheartedly that angels came to town, for it's changed him. "I've adopted a dog and I'm a better father to my daughter now. I started a business thanks to my extended family." But then he says something so thrilling, no one has ever mentioned it. No, he doesn't speak of Emma Rose, his daughter seeing angels. No, he speaks of his dog, Bondo. "Bondo looks up in the sky on some nights when we take our walk. Then when we get home he loves to look out my second story apartment window for a while. I track his eyes. These are not birds he's watching. No, I feel certain they are angels. Madam Norma told me we all have a guardian angel and she feels they are here and fly at night when no one can see. I think animals definitely can see angels!"

July feigns surprise. "Jamie, this is wonderful. You have brought an incredible piece into this discussion on our show today! Do animals see angels? I'd like to think they do!" Of course July knows full well they see us. Every time we fly the dogs and cats of town watch us if they're outside. Even Bubbles the funny squirrel sees us and cocks his head, then starts chattering. Gabe took Bubbles flying once and it was beyond hysterical to see. "Wide-eyed and bushytailed," Gabe says.

Laurjean is next to come up on stage talking about fostering and how she knows it was all angel inspired. Today she wears her most colorful clothes ever, a gold sweater and gold lame slacks, gold heels and a slight gold streak in her hair. I love this naturally funny and fun woman. She's the dear wife of Donnie, my angel friend and the world's best angel secret keeper. I have to keep a straight face when she says, "Land sakes, dogs seeing angels. That's so right on! It's true our old dog, Chuck, sees something in the night's sky. I bet its angels. All I know is I love this town. I'm so glad we adopted our son. It's made me a better person, too. So many here have adopted and fostered kids and adopted animals. Older folks are helping the homeless in San Francisco and my husband helps with the Bay Area Sports Program for kids in group homes and shelters. Yes, there are little miracles happening here every day thanks to the angels."

We go to break for a commercial and all the guests leave the chairs but July and Noah. It's going well. When the show is back on air, the service man, Ted, from the angel debate talks about his drowning incident where he didn't see the angel but an angel pulled him to shore and saved his life.

But then July has a surprise! Klaus Waxman is the next guest! He walks up to her on the gazebo and shakes Noah's hand. He also shakes Teds' and Julys' hands. "Everyone, this is a story that prompted our angel debates in town last year. Klaus Waxman was a storeowner for a short while in town. You challenged us all to an angel debate. Please tell us what you gleaned from the debate."

Klaus looks nervous and I'm taken aback that he would ask to be on the show. He looks better. He's dressed nicely and his demeanor has changed.

"July, I came to town to open a store to bully the townspeople and certain individuals. My life had been hard throughout and I didn't believe in psychics or angels. I was a lawyer and would help my fellow man, but when it came to my personal life, well, I made a complete mess of it.

Out of anger, I asked for an angel debate and heard these stories that have been told here today.

But that's not what changed my mind, July. You see it was all the people of Mystic Bay. Madam Norma, my dear departed friend, spoke kindly to me. Before she passed away she had already found me a new mentor, a man that shall remain anonymous for various reasons. Kindness is what changed me, the kindness of the people in Mystic Bay. I don't know if I believe in angels but I believe in angel traits especially here in Mystic Bay. And I'd like to apologize to all those I've hurt along the way. I'm sorry. I acted like a fool, but no more."

It's quiet in the crowd. July is kind and thanks him for his honesty. He stays seated next to her. Relief is on his face. "And now everyone, a most joyous occasion for us. Benny Chen is here. He is the boy who the angels visited in the night. They sang a song for him to play for us. The angels told Benny the song was to be called, *Forever Peace, Forever Love.* As we leave you now with this most beautiful song, remember in Riverton to the south of Mystic Bay is *The Angel Museum* where you can hear Benny's rendition of the song throughout the day. The song is played at wedding, funerals and all kinds of celebrations. The museum is free to the public and you can also see the paintings inspired by the angels. The artwork recently returned from a yearlong worldwide tour. I leave you with the angel song as we all call it. Thank you to all my guests. Noah, best of luck with your documentary. I can't wait to see it, as we all will be waiting! Thank you all!"

He's at the piano, the child prodigy, Benny Chen. His father, Anthony, plays the violin and the San Francisco Symphony plays with him. So many in the crowd close their eyes to the most beautiful song ever played. It's as beautiful as children's laughter and the feeling of love. I open my eyes and look up. On every rooftop they stand side by side. The town is full of angels, some guardian angels and some healing angels. All the angels in the nearby areas are gathered to witness the show. The world is watching and listening. Perhaps there will be more sightings.

Perhaps a door has been opened. Perhaps there is a spiritual awakening coming. And yet I know in my angel heart, there already is.

Chapter 23

Autumn Begins Again

I'm walking in the afternoon sun. It's one of those beautiful fall days at the California seaside that make us all, angel and human alike, more grateful for the life we've been given. Even though we seven angels keep thankfulness in our hearts, we feel even more joyous than ever having a human experience.

Klaus bought a house on July and January's street. His view of the Pacific is almost as spectacular as his neighbor, *The Sea Watch Hotel's* view. He's fully retired now and I haven't seen him in a month. He's been overly busy with his move and his retirement. We decided to always meet once a month. We meet on Tuesdays at Madam Norma's. Of course we will always call it her house though now it's Tim and Miss Marilyn's home. They are so welcoming to us and Mabel and King seem to enjoy being with us too. We have become very fond of them.

Klaus wants me to see his new house and I think next time I may invite him over to mine. He thinks I've never been here but, of course, I have. The seven of us flew one night from July's rooftop and before we went sailing on the wind with angel wings spreading to the shine of the moon, we stopped for a moment witnessing Klaus standing on his patio overlooking the sea. We found him using his new telescope observing the star filled heavens. He's a changed man. Whoever said a leopard doesn't change his spots was wrong. People can change because of free will. We call him the 'Comeback Kid Two' for he is another of Madam Norma's changed men, like lovable and ever maturing,

Jamie Bond.

He meets me at the door and I walk into a big yet unpretentious home. With many boxes still unopened, I find his dog, Lucky, right by his side and Dot curled and curious lying on the little table to the side of the door. "Come in Ken," he says with a smile. He's lost weight and the drawn look is gone from his face. "Can I get you some tea? I made it and bought us some banana bread from *The Mystic Bay Bakery.* It's not as good as Maggie's, but it'll do."

I tell him yes of course as we walk into the sprawling house with its comfy chairs and light and airy feel. "Let's sit in the study. The view is gorgeous. It's a little chilly to sit outside right now." I sit and we chat awhile and I see an inner peace has come to him. He's a man who has resolved many of his issues.

"I miss our weekly talks and I wondered… well, I'll tell you more in a little while. Would you like tea?"

"Yes. Thank you kindly." I'm still amazed at the change in him seeing him in his new home environment.

"We sit and have our tea and he asks about Val's beginning school days and then he says a most remarkable thing.

"Would you be willing to help a friend of mine? He's a man I met in AA. I really think he could use your kind influence and your stories of angels. I know you're busy with Val and the sports program. And I'm offering to volunteer as much as you need me with your Bay Area Sports Program."

I'm overwhelmed, my angel heart is grateful for seeing this man's growing and giving heart.

"Of course, yes, I'd be happy to meet with your friend. And thank you so much, we need more hands in the sports program. There are so many kids who need us."

"Great, you could meet him with me at first. We could meet here if you'd like. His name is Paul. "

"Yes, Klaus. I'm touched you asked me."

"Ken, I need to know again, and I've asked you before, we all have a guardian angel, you are sure of it? "

"Yes, I really do believe it, Klaus."

"And you think Madam Norma and Freddy and Tyrone are always with me?"

"I'm as sure as the rain falls, that is true."

"Have you seen Madam Norma's spirit?"

"Why yes, I have, but only for a moment." He is asking me so many questions and of course angels never lie.

It's then he says something to me that makes me almost disappear from sight. It happens to angels when they are overwhelmed with sadness, humanly fear or surprise. And right now, suddenly, I am a little fearful. I feel my wings urging to sprout and nervousness sets in.

"I believe you're an angel, Ken, and that you don't want anyone to know. I believe God sent you here to help Val and me and so many others. I watch you. You almost glow and some days you actually appear bigger. That man, Cliff, at the angel debate? He said you were the spitting image of the man who helped him on that dangerous curve years ago. You laughed it away but I could tell you were visibly shaken. And then at the Town of Angels TV Show when he was interviewed, he didn't mention how the man that day looked like you. He totally glossed it over. You are well known so why didn't he say it? It was very strange.

He told us all he thought the man who helped him had to be an angel. Why, I've wondered didn't he bring your name up on July's show. It got me thinking about you. Could I be right? Could you tell me? Are you a real angel? I'd never tell if it's true, I promise! It would help me so much to know for sure."

I sit glued to the chair not knowing how to respond. My wings want to pop out but I try to control them. He opens up the sliding glass door and beckons me to walk outside with him. We are standing looking out at the sea when he begins again.

"And then that day when you showed up at *DiMaggio's Place* in the morning? How did you know I was there? Did you fly there?" He turns to me again. "Madam Norma said you know more about angels then anyone. She said also that you see them. Did she know you were an angel Ken? I need to know."

I am speechless. I hold my wings back with my angel mind and they stop sprouting. Not noticing anything odd he continues. I sit on the chaise across the balcony from him. I start to speak but he puts up his hand.

"Listen, you are the finest man I've ever known in my life. Knowing you are an angel would help me get through my life and it would be a secret I would keep. I swear." Klaus looks at me with tears in his eyes. Thankfully, my composure comes. The Lord gives me the words.

"If I'm an angel, then I'm only an angel to some. It's an honor to me you think of me as an angel. Thank you."

It's then I see her, Madam Norma. She's smiling behind him, standing in a blue dress looking younger still. I see Lucky and Dot stare at her. In an instant she is gone. I decide quickly to communicate wordlessly to the animals to go to Klaus for a hug. "Run," I tell them with my mind. Kindheart, his angel stands near to us now. He nods smiling. The dog and cat look at the angel and then at me and run to Klaus almost flying into his arms. Klaus smiles and laughs at big Lucky almost bowling him over. He surely is about to say more to me but I send him angel dust with a slight wave of my hand. It covers him from head to toe with little silvery sparkles he can't see. Lucky and Dot see them and Dot unsuccessfully paws at them. Klaus closes his eyes then opens them again. Hopefully, it's worked.

"What was I saying? Oh, yes I was telling you about my friend,

Paul. It's indeed nice of you to help him. I know he'll learn so much from you. I was saying something else I don't remember what. Oh yes, Madam Norma was like an angel!" He smiles again.

"Yes, she was an angel to me too." Looking out to the sun's glimmer on the salty sea, I take in a big angel breath. That was close. My being an angel must be kept a secret.

I realize then, too, that Klaus didn't notice my form changing. Even if he thinks about me being an angel again, it will only be a passing thought. The angel dust has done its job.

"I miss her. Do you think I might get to see her spirit some day?"

"Oh yes, it is totally possible, Klaus!" I look at the man who no one thought would ever change as he holds his dog and cat near. Life is good for him in so many ways. He's being firm with his daughter and just maybe somehow it will help her. He's found the goodness in his soul.

"Ask her to come to you and maybe someday she will." I stand then walking over to look out at the ocean taking in God's beautiful earth and sea. The endless waves and salty wind make me want to fly right this very minute but I know regrettably, I have to wait until nightfall. I breathe a deep angel human breath and turn to him, "Always ask the angels for everything you need."

It's then I decide to send him butterflies; just a few and they appear suddenly swirling by him. As quickly as they come they fly away. However, I signal one pretty small yellow one. It flies to his shoulder. He stares at it for a moment then looks at me. The animals don't move. I communicate to them to be still. The butterfly flies away.

"Did you see that Ken? A butterfly just landed on my shoulder. It's like the butterfly paintings Justine paints for her store's window, those beautiful paintings where butterflies have landed on people and animals! I can't believe it! How awesome is that?"

I sigh. "Yes, Klaus, my dear friend. Justine is such a talented psychic. She tells me that butterflies come to us only on the sweetest of days!"

Dear Reader,

I thank you for reading Town of Angels. I believe I might have met an angel in human form once long ago after my daughter, Kate, passed away. I have known people who I believe are like angels on earth. These angels unaware help the down trodden and everyone with their kindness. To my friends, my former students, and kind strangers, all angels unaware, I am eternally grateful. Angels give me inspiration in my daydreams and dreams. I am sure of this for heaven sent this story for me to write. It's a story of love, joy, forgiveness, hope and kindness. I believe kindness is the truest expression of love.

Jody Sharpe

Acknowledgements

It is with gratitude and humbleness I thank the following people for believing in my work. I thank my Editor extraordinaire, writer, Patty Mahoney, who edited my novels, To Catch an Angel and Town of Angels. I'd like to thank Don McCauley, my Publicist, for his amazing talent, vision, hard work, patience and kindness. Michael Zara and Elizabeth Alexandre, my twins, I thank for their special love and encouragement. I have many friends who supported me along the way with their enduring friendship. I am thankful for my dear friend, Nancy Astrom, who with a kind heart took me on a girl's trip to Houston, Texas with her after my daughter, Kate, passed away. There we are sure we encountered an angel.

I'd like to thank my dear husband, Dave Moskowitz, who changed my life by being a wonderful friend for many years, and now my rock, life partner and kindred spirit.

Lastly, I will always thank the unnamed angel I'm sure Nancy and I met on our trip to Houston. It's been over twenty years now but I know he came for a moment in my life to comfort me by materializing, giving me the courage to move forward with joy and hope. He became the inspiration for the Mystic Bay Series where angels live as humans in a town where no one knows the secret.